LEXI GREENE

Bachelor on Guard

First published by Warrior Heart Publishing 2020

This novel is entirely a work of fiction. The names, characters and incidents portrayed in it are the work of the author's imagination. Any resemblance to actual persons, living or dead, events or localities is entirely coincidental.

Lexi Greene asserts the moral right to be identified as the author of this work.

First edition

ISBN: 978-0-6483874-8-0

This book was professionally typeset on Reedsy.
Find out more at reedsy.com

Foreword

Abby Kercher has spent the past five years proving she doesn't need Nico D'Antoni, but now her life is in danger and Nico is the only man who can keep her safe.

Abby is all grown up and Nico finds she's changed in dangerous ways, but some things haven't changed, like their unwanted attraction, the darkness of his past, and his promise to protect her, which must override everything.

Can they put their past behind them, or will a long-kept secret destroy them both?

Acknowledgement

Thank you to my brilliant editor, Jena O'Connor from Practical Proofing and my fabulous cover designer, Charmaine Ross. And thank you to Romance Writers of Australia and Romance Writers of America for your support and guidance. And a huge thank you to Beverley Eikli and Nina Campbell for your endless inspiration, awesome feedback, and wise words.

Prologue

Long Bay Correctional Centre, NSW, Australia

The air was sweeter on the outside. Raffaele D'Antoni took a deep breath and closed his eyes to better savour the blissful caress of freedom. His suit hung loose around him and with every step, his dress shoes squeezed the sensitive flesh of his feet. His stomach growled and his eyes snapped open. What he wouldn't give for a meat pie with sauce, and a beer. He walked down the short, wire-fenced driveway towards Anzac Parade, soaking up the warmth of the winter sun.

The pleasure of walking was marred by his limp. His shoes hurt like a bitch. He'd lost weight on the inside, but more than that, he'd lost his self-respect. Funny how a man could be stripped away and reconstructed in a place like that. Reconstructed in a way that didn't seem to fit with the world around him.

Sleek, shiny cars zipped past, with a crisp whooshing sound. A woman walked along the path on the opposite side of the road pushing a pram, a strangely shaped contraption that looked more like a trolley. He shaded his eyes with his hand to better appreciate the glade of eucalyptus trees and the green of the grass.

With every step, his tension eased, only to be stoked again by the barrage of sounds. He turned towards Maroubra. Before his detention, three kilometres was child's play. Now, his heart pounded, and his blood warmed despite the slight chill in the air. He wanted that pie and beer, and then he wanted revenge.

He should have been living the good life. If it hadn't been for Dominico—his insides twisted, and his blood roared in his ears at just the thought of his younger brother—he'd have banked his share of the ransom money and earned his father's respect. And if Lorenzo, the dog, hadn't sexually assaulted the woman in front of her kid, which was never part of the plan, Raffaele wouldn't have rotted in the slammer for a full twenty years. No way was he ever going back. He'd rather be dead.

Worse, his brother got rich, thanks to Bob Kercher and his billions. That money should have been his. Every step hammered another nail into Dominico's coffin... he would pay for what he stole. Dominico thought he was better and smarter than the brother he'd betrayed. Well, Raffaele planned to expose him for the charlatan he was. Remind him of his roots. Whoever said that blood was thicker than water was wrong. His brother's blood was thin. Thin on loyalty. Thin on respect. Thin on what mattered.

A car sped past with a rush of cool air, and Raffaele checked his position on the verge of the road. It wouldn't do to get killed now. Not after all he'd suffered. All he'd survived. No, he had a job to do and a debt to repay. His skin puckered and pulled, every follicle clenching. Bruno wasn't a rational man, and his sexual interest in children was... perverse. Raffaele's nose screwed up. But the job ticked more boxes than the swag of cash he'd make and the debt he'd clear. A debt he owed because of Dominico and his interference. Bruno hadn't forgotten his missed opportunity with the little posh princess—and what an irony that she'd grown up to be a royal pain in Bruno's arse. Raffaele smirked.

But he'd gladly kill her for no reason other than to get back at Bob Kercher for feathering his brother's nest. A win-win. A win for Raffaele's reputation amongst his bikie mates—and he had some making up to do—and a win for his own goal: payback.

He'd learned a thing or two sucking on the teat of the mother of all murderers... he steeled his spine and pulled his jacket more tightly around the broken pieces of the man he used to be. With four weeks until the trial in Bangkok, he had plenty of time to take out Lorenzo, head down to Melbourne to deal with Abigail Kercher, and then the most satisfying of all, Dominico.

Raffaele turned and glared at the walls he'd left behind. He couldn't fail. He wouldn't fail. And nothing would give him more pleasure than to see his brother dead. He took a deep breath of the wintry air and hitched his pants.

A crow cawed—loud and raucous and sharp—the sound slashing through the cacophony of other sounds that bombarded his ears like a foreign language after twenty years in the slammer courtesy of his younger brother.

Revenge would be sweet. Sweeter than a peep show. Better than sex. That was a thought that used to stir his nether regions. Yet another loss to lay at the foot of his damn brother.

Chapter One

Abby Kercher was all grown up. No sign of the twenty-year old femme fatale who'd haunted Nico's sleep for the past five years.

He leaned back against the wall of the ballroom at the Grand Hyatt Hotel in Melbourne, preferring the quiet sanctuary of his shadowy corner to the light of the glittering function room.

He couldn't equate the self-assured dynamo who'd just stepped down from the stage to massive applause with the naïve, indulged, daddy's princess he'd safeguarded from a discreet distance while she'd kicked up her killer heels and razed the Sydney social scene. Bob's mentorship and support had been a blessing, especially in the early days of Nico's security business, but the job of protecting his precious teenage daughter had not.

This woman was poised, intelligent and humble. Beautiful, yes, but in an understated, quiet, grow-on-you kind of way; a far cry from the designer-clad brat, all sexy pout and barely out of school, who'd propositioned him with such wanton disregard for his professional reputation.

He watched as she circulated, serenely confident, politely aloof, oblivious to the sweep of male eyes as she moved with ease from person to person. Her black dress brought images

4

of Audrey Hepburn—classic but smoking hot—to that part of his brain that still harboured memories of her scent, the feel of her in his arms, her lush, perfect mouth a whisper from his. Innocent, naïve, and foolish was what she'd been.

He stepped into the light as she circulated closer, anticipation like fire in his veins. Far from in distress, she looked like a damsel very unlikely to welcome his interference in her security arrangements. Death threats and her father's blessing aside, he doubted Abby Kercher would play a willing role in her own disappearance.

"Ah, Mr. D'Antoni. I believe we owe you an enormous thanks."

Sea-green eyes collided with his and his heart stalled. Edges flashed like shards of glass behind the polite veneer. So, she hadn't forgotten his less-than-careful rejection. Her smile was warm enough, albeit surface-deep across a chasm of well-mannered distance. Her hair was drawn back into a demure knot at the nape of her neck. His memories were very clear on her siren-like hair—auburn, burnished locks with golden highlights, long and full, silken and soft. Memories of its glorious scent charged back; thick and fast. His gaze dropped to her lips... shiny with pink gloss. They looked wet and plump and one hundred percent kissable.

What the hell was he thinking? Bob had hired him to help, not to hinder, but Bob had no idea what a temptress his daughter had been.

"If it wasn't for the generosity of people such as yourself, Project Karma wouldn't come close to being able to achieve what it does." Her professional mask fitted like a second skin and Nico scrambled to fortify his own.

There was no sign of the sexual sorcery she'd wielded like

a weapon. Nothing to justify the visceral-deep reaction that slammed through him at just the touch of her hand on his arm. Her movement was instinctive and retracted before he'd had time to catch his breath... unlike her lingering touches of old.

The old Abby was resistible. The new Abby was like an undetonated hand grenade.

He hot-wired his vocal cords and found his voice. "My money has gone to an excellent cause. Your work is admirable." He, too, could feign civilised. Indeed, he'd made it an art form.

"Thank you." She looked at him with a faintly perplexed crease in her brow. Had her thoughts shifted to the unlikely coincidence that the CEO of D'Antoni Security services—her former bodyguard—should reappear in her life within twenty-four hours of the televised feature documentary about Project Karma and the heist, not twelve months ago, that had led to the deaths of four undercover operatives. The operation had saved dozens of children from criminal exploitation and exposed a major paedophile ring, but retribution had come thick and fast.

Her survival had been kept from the media—the thought of how close she'd come to dying clawed at his insides. Her testimony would be vital in the pending trial that would see the perpetrators imprisoned for life.

It wasn't safe for her in Bangkok, and now, thanks to the documentary, it wasn't safe for her in Melbourne. The Project Karma charity office had received a death threat targeting Abby's life within minutes of the show finishing.

If Bob Kercher hadn't asked for a personal favour, if Nico hadn't owed Bob more than he could repay in a lifetime, he would never have agreed to his current assignment. The less time spent around Abby Kercher the better for his physical and mental health.

Abby's gaze pierced right through him and he shifted uncomfortably in his Italian leather shoes. Did she see the bad boy behind the civilised front? She didn't know him well enough. No woman did.

"How many people are here tonight?" He steered her attention towards the room.

"One thousand, one hundred and fifty-four." There was pride and satisfaction in her tone, and a lofty grace in her stance as she turned to survey the splendour of the scene before them.

At fifteen hundred dollars a ticket that added up to a tidy sum, before she even started on the donations and pledges, which would come thick and fast after her impressive speech and heart-wrenching slideshow.

"You must be very happy with the turn out."

Her attention shifted back, and her smile took the light in her eyes to a new dimension, igniting spot-fires all over his body.

"It's better than I could have hoped for and it will further our work. There's still so much to be done."

He observed the passion that flared in her eyes and realised with a jolt that she really cared, which surprised him. The young woman he'd trailed with such disdain had been a spoiled little rich girl more interested in shopping for shoes and handbags than sparing a thought for those less fortunate. The only people he could have imagined less worthy of his time were the two young women she'd called friends. Self-centred prima donnas more like.

"I heard about your ordeal." That your life was in danger—*is* in danger. Again.

"Yes." Her gaze veered away from his.

She'd point-blank refused his personal protection since the night of her wayward proposition. That had ended badly, but not as badly as her overseas jaunt to Thailand. Not too many young women landed themselves in as much trouble as Abby had. The thought of her experience was a jagged edge to his conscience. It might never have happened if he'd handled the situation better. At twenty-seven, he'd been aggressive and hell-bent on building an empire. A dalliance with Abby Kercher would have threatened all that he wanted to achieve. Besides, money could do a lot of things, but it couldn't change the black blood that coursed in his veins. Nor could it change the fact that Abby was Bob's daughter. Bob knew exactly where Nico's roots lay, and it wasn't any place worthy of his precious daughter.

Abby moved with ease in the upper echelons of Sydney society or at least she had.

Yet, here she was, in Melbourne, fighting for a cause he couldn't help but admire. Many tourists saw the seedy side of Bangkok but not many put a dent in the child sex trade industry.

The woman by his side was all mature sophistication and far from the femme fatale who relentlessly graced the boudoir of his dreams. Well, not in any complete way. More in a myriad of pixels—her hair, her scent, the soft press of her breasts against his chest, her body lithe and twisted around him like a velvet bind. He shook the sensual torment from his head.

The volume of her voice dropped. "I guess you know about the trial." He didn't miss the defiance that sharpened her tone. She was on to him.

"I heard you plan to testify." And put your life in a ridiculous amount of danger.

"Is that so unbelievable?" Her siren-green eyes clashed with his as surely as two swords crossing blades. There was steel behind the porcelain doll front and it took him a moment to recover from the shock.

"I can identify the perpetrators involved and keep them behind bars. That's more important than staying safe. Besides, I have protection. Protection *I* pay for." She nodded towards a fellow in black who lurked nearby, his earpiece readily visible.

The bad element involved in the trade of children into Thai brothels wouldn't hesitate to kill her. "The Abby I remember would have balked at a broken fingernail."

"I'm not that girl anymore." Her eyes glistened. She had him at a disadvantage. His brain just couldn't catch up.

"You were involved in the heist that rescued those kids?"

"Yes, but after… after what happened, I took on a paid role in Melbourne coordinating our fund-raising events." Her back was stiff, and her chin lifted to challenge his height advantage.

"We need to talk." His tone softened to an encouraging purr. "If not tonight, then first thing tomorrow morning." If he'd hoped for cooperation, he'd have been disappointed.

Her kidnap had been carefully planned. He was the kind of man who paid attention to the details. Like the slight hesitation before her smile recovered and the flare in the size of her pupils before her lashes lowered to hide them, her gaze raking over him. She'd like what she saw he was certain of that. When her eyes returned to his, the small giveaway was carefully masked, her manners as polished as the fine crystal glasses and silver cutlery.

"Thank you, but I have other plans."

He took her rebuff with gentlemanly grace. *Her* plans were

of no consequence. They were to board a private jet in the early afternoon the next day, and he had the full collaboration of the witness protection program and a directive from her father.

The set of her shoulders and the steel in her spine told him she wouldn't make his job easy. She didn't want his protection, Bob had implied as much, but the security people she'd hired were lightweights. Nico eyed the fellow who stood out from the crowd, his gaze shifting from Abby to the wider room.

Bob had assured him that while Abby presented a brave front, she wasn't as brave on the inside. She'd suffered nightmares for years following her abduction at Raffaele's hands. Nico's skin tightened and his fist curled. Raffaele's prison term was nearly up, and their day of reckoning was coming, but if Nico had his time again? He locked eyes with Abby's defiant ones. He'd make the same call.

Abby had been five years old… and beyond terrified. He shuddered as he thought of how close she'd come to being violated. Even at twelve, he'd understood what his brother's mate, Bruno, had in mind.

Abby excused herself and moved away. Nico leaned back against the wall and watched her mingle with the crowd, her face lit with the kind of smile that grabbed a man by the balls.

She still didn't know the truth about what had happened, and Bob had made Nico promise she wouldn't hear about it from him, but the truth sat restlessly in his stomach like an oyster left too long in the sun. She'd been too young to remember and Bob had told her it was a bad dream. Not real.

She should be safe here, but what if she wasn't? He couldn't stop the spider-like creep of ice along his spine.

His instincts were usually spot-on, but Abby messed with

his radar.

With a murmur into a small mic on his lapel, he alerted his team.

'Don't let her out of your sight. Where this woman goes, trouble isn't far behind.'

Nico's piercing blue gaze bore an uncomfortable hole in the centre of Abby's back. If time hadn't erased the disturbing effect he had on her, then humiliation should have. Nowhere in her fantasies of their reunion had she not flayed him with her haughty gaze and made it black-and-white clear that her teenage crush was dust-in-the-wind gone. Ashes to ashes. But the size of his pledge had left her torn between gratitude and the desire to scratch out those hellion eyes.

Why was he here?

Nico's actions were always by design and he was meticulous with details. She of all people knew that. His attendance at this shindig was suspicious at best. Well, he could rest assured that she was a woman in charge. No sign of her mother's affliction. And if he was here on her father's behalf, he could take that message back, loud and clear. She didn't need his protection. She didn't want it. She wouldn't tolerate it.

She lifted a champagne glass from a passing tray, and took a tiny sip, the bubbles bursting and tickling her nose. Her pulse was an edgy throb, and her body was wound as tight as if she'd pulled up onto her toes and planted her lips on his. Nico's effect on her had nothing to do with his lofty position on the BRW rich list, although she recognised the expensive cut of his suit and the fine quality of the fabric. His money didn't impress her so much as the fact that he'd built his empire from nothing. The man was a force. A force who'd taken her down and taught her a lesson or six.

Her own outfit had cost more than a week's salary, but it was worth it. If she wanted to mix with the rich and famous, she had to look the part. She greeted a lovely older couple and asked if they were enjoying the evening, but Nico's gaze burned into her skin like a brand—still. Did he have nothing better to do than stare?

Nico may have pledged a substantial sum, but she wasn't part of the deal. It should be enough to know his money would help rescue innocent children from a terrible fate.

Yet for a moment, she'd been sorely tempted to meet with him. To show she could face him adult-to-adult and have a mature conversation with no sign of her embarrassing affliction, but the embers of her teenage crush had flared into blistering life and wiped out five years of hard work.

His gaze was like a laser on her back. Flames licked along her spine and heat unfurled in her abdomen leaving her antsy and distracted. She moved on to another group engaged in a lively conversation, but she struggled to find her equilibrium and before she knew it, she was back in Nico's orbit.

"You've gone full circle."

And there he was. The deep timbre of his voice stirred the fine hairs on her skin and sent her pulse racing. She tightened her grip on her champagne glass. "Has no one ever told you it's rude to stare?"

So much for keeping her cool. There was nothing cool about the way her body reacted to Nico's devoted scrutiny. He was even more gorgeous than she remembered. His olive-skinned complexion looked striking against the whiteness of his shirt; his jawline was square and peppered with sexy man-shadow, and some traitorous part of her longed to run her fingers through his dark, short-cropped hair. He oozed confidence from every pore and his musky male scent filled her head with crazy teenage longings. Smouldering and intense, his eyes sapped the strength from her bones. Or maybe it was his mega-watt smile, all white teeth and killer dimples. Mischievous. Devil-may-care-dangerous. Criminal in her wretched opinion.

"Isn't that why women dress the way they do? To get a man's attention?"

The intensity of his gaze had far from tempered, and Abby couldn't stop the flush that invaded her body with unwelcome heat. She sipped her drink and resisted the urge to rest the cold glass against her burning cheeks. His arrogance knew no bounds.

"It's a black-tie event. Women dress up to feel glamorous and confident." How could she have let his mockery get to her? 'Perhaps you'd be so kind as to direct your attention to one of the many beautiful women in attendance tonight who might welcome it?' She glanced around the room as if to underscore her point.

"I would have thought it a small liberty..." His blue eyes glittered, and she shivered despite the warmth of the heating. "Given our history."

How dare he bring up her less-than-salubrious, ill-conceived proposition? The fire that incinerated her insides razed her cheeks. She'd long ago relegated him to her don't-go-there box and unceremoniously dumped the key.

"Nico, whilst I appreciate your very sizeable donation, if you think your money buys you any personal favours, you can think again." She infused her tone with back-off. Why was he here? To take up her misguided offer after all these years?

Over her dead body.

"Perhaps I owe you an apology, Abby." His tone was conciliatory, but her name on his tongue was a liberty she'd rather have denied him.

"And I really would like to speak with you in a different setting."

Abby stifled a frustrated scream with a slow sip of her champagne. He'd managed to manoeuvre her into the awkward position of having to refuse his invitation again, and her mind had gone blank of polite platitudes.

"No perhaps about it." She went to move away but his hand snaked out and stilled her, his palm searing her skin, sending an electric charge along her hypersensitive nerve endings. She lifted her eyes to his with warning and he loosened his grip as if surprised by the contact. What was it about Nico that left her witless and nervy, and much worse—weak?

"I apologise."

Was it her imagination or was there veiled amusement in his eyes? Abby shook off the disturbing effect of his touch.

"Apology accepted. Enjoy the rest of your evening." She accompanied her words with a forced smile and moved away with purpose like there was somewhere she needed to be. Her head throbbed and fatigue dragged at her limbs… she wound her way to the ladies' bathroom, where she did her best to pull herself together. She needed a good night's sleep, not punctuated by nightmares and cold sweats.

She was more worried about the approaching trial than she liked to admit. She wanted the perpetrators punished for their crime, but did she really want to risk her life? The others were dead. All of them. And the fact that she'd survived was more testament to Gary's quick thinking than her own. He'd saved her life.

Damn her father for being so melodramatic. The thought of returning to Bangkok brought hives to her skin. She smoothed fresh gloss over her lips and decided she'd leave as soon as her commitments allowed it. Nico's presence was like a pall over her, and the effort of appearing confident and resilient in the face of her excruciating memories was taking its toll.

Dessert was being served by the time she left the sanctuary of the bathroom and made her way back to her table. She'd eat and then make her excuses. Thanks to Nico D'Antoni, she didn't have to feign a pounding headache.

But when she returned to her seat, she had a new companion. The man himself and his face lit up as she approached.

"Oh, there you are. I was worried you might miss the white chocolate mousse cake and raspberries, which I must say are outstanding. You certainly haven't short-changed your guests on the food front."

"Suggesting I have short-changed them on some other front?"

He was like a piece of grit in her eye. Abrasive. Annoying. But at this juncture, unavoidable. She sank into her seat with reluctant resignation.

"None that I'm aware of." His tone was bright, and he was every bit the charming and friendly dinner companion. He drew everyone around the table into lively conversation. She listened with disbelief as he effortlessly charmed and wooed the other women. He was never short of a date if gossip was to be believed, which brought her thoughts back to his invitation. What was his game-plan?

With coffee finalised, she began to make her farewells.

What had begun as a throbbing headache had taken on the

proportions of a migraine.

Nico's uncomfortable proximity hadn't helped. He'd more than once consulted her opinion on a topic and had exaggerated the level of intimacy between them.

But whatever devious plan he had in mind… she was about to stonewall it.

"Thank you all for coming tonight, and please enjoy the rest of your evening." She smiled graciously at the others seated at her table and picked up her wrap. The black silk was taken from her hands before she'd had time to tighten her grip and Nico settled it around her shoulders.

She reached for her bag and he made to accompany her.

"Nico, there's no need for you to leave. Please stay and enjoy the rest of the evening. I think the others are going on to a nightclub."

"Oh, I have an early start tomorrow." His gaze snagged hers and the undercurrent in his tone lifted the hair follicles on her skin.

"Well, I won't keep you then."

"Perhaps you'd like a lift home? It's rather late to find a taxi."

"Thank you, but no. I'll wait with the concierge if there isn't one ready to go. It was lovely to see you again." As lovely as having teeth pulled. "Please don't rush on my account." Her smile was less than skin deep. The man was infuriating. Most men's egos were fragile enough to keep their distance when met with resistance, but Nico it seemed was made of sterner stuff.

"Perhaps we should share a cab, and then I'll know you've made it home safely." His words were bright, but she felt like a mouse skewered in the sights of an eagle. It didn't matter which way she turned; he was there at every exit.

"You're most kind, but that won't be necessary. My security service will ensure I make it home safely." She was no mouse and if he thought he could bully her into acquiescence, he was wrong.

Abby walked with precise, determined steps towards the exit and away from the charming, persistent, attentive man whose stare even now sent sizzling messages to her senses. The last thing she wanted was to lose herself in those cerulean blue eyes and bow to his domination. Her independence had been too hard won.

Chapter Two

I f Nico had wanted to kill Abby, he'd have had numerous opportunities. Clear shots. With a silencer, had he wound down the window of the car, she'd be dead, and he'd have disappeared into the Sunday traffic along the beach front and no one would have known where the bullet had come from.

And where was her security detail? Paid off without so much as a whimper. Nico had spent an uncomfortable night in his car, keeping watch over her house. Maybe he should have shadowed her on foot and got some exercise himself. They had a long trip ahead.

Running along Beaconsfield Parade towards Port Melbourne, albeit amongst a throng of people, was not keeping safe.

Keeping safe was staying inside behind locked doors, although if he could find her Middle Park address with such little difficulty, so could anyone. The small hawthorn brick terrace house had surprised him. He'd figured her for the glossy penthouse apartment type. The front had been tidy; the small garden beautifully tended.

Nico pulled into the traffic, keeping Abby in his line of sight. The wind pulled at the determined walkers and runners, and he knew the chill factor had to be high. The bay was furious, the waves churning and smashing against the white sand. He watched Abby as she deviated from the concrete running track onto the grassy verge to bypass a young girl on a scooter, her pink helmet a bright dot against the low-slung bluestone wall. A row of date palms stretched in orderly fashion along the length of the foreshore, their tops torn and buffeted by the wind. Kite surfers leapt out of the water, suspended in the air, until their boards arrowed back into the chop with speed and power.

He could see the appeal.

Nico edged the prestige hire-car into a parking bay on the side of the road and watched Abby in the rear-view mirror. She made steady progress along the lengthy promenade. Her long hair was pulled back into a ponytail—a gloriously thick one that bounced with each jogging step that she took. She wore black leggings and a t-shirt and had wires leading to both ears, suggesting she was listening to music.

Nico rolled his eyes. She had not the first clue about snipers. She needed every sense on alert, not obliterated by thumping music.

He should stop her before someone else did. It would be simple enough for someone to pull a trigger as they walked past her. Observers would think she'd tripped or had a heart attack. No one would realise she'd been shot until it was too late to identify the culprit. There'd be no witnesses. No lead to follow.

He gritted his teeth.

To abduct her in broad daylight was fraught.

She was not the quiet type. Nor had he figured her for the type to be up early on a Sunday morning and out jogging in the crisp cold air.

Why she couldn't have allowed him the opportunity to explain the situation he'd never know. It didn't need to be this dramatic. But it was urgent. She was likely being followed. At best, observed. For now.

According to Bob, she would never consent to his protection. After last night, he'd have to agree. He'd met resistance at every turn. Polite, sugar-coated, steely resistance. How was he to keep her safe when she was unwilling to go into hiding and thought her fool security detail was up to the job?

His brief was impossible, but he'd overcome greater odds. Surprise was the best route to success. Not the route he would have chosen, given her likely furious reaction, but necessary.

Hopefully, there'd be no need to use the weapon he had secreted away for safety's sake.

Nico moved into the turning lane and with Abby still visible in his rear-view mirror, he drove at a more normal speed and parked not far from her house. Abby would be sure to head in now. She'd been running for over an hour.

Standing under a tree, he waited for her to progress along the path. She'd need a shower. He hadn't thought of that but there was one on their private jet. She'd just have to tidy up once they were in the air.

He stepped out and blocked her path.

"Abby. What a pleasant surprise."

"Nico." His name on her tongue was breathy and high pitched with shock. "What are you doing here?"

Immediately on the attack. "Waiting for you."

"Why?"

"I need you to come with me and time is of the essence. I'll explain in the car."

"No, thank you." He had to laugh, even as he cursed her

father for putting him in such an awkward position. He was a protector; he was not in the habit of abducting young women who politely refused to cooperate, and his task was an odious one.

"I insist." He closed both of his hands around her slender arms and looked into her cantankerous green eyes, his voice dropping in volume. "You have a choice here. You can come willingly, or you can come under duress but come you will. You're not safe. Now, which way is it going to be?"

Abby's stance was defiant, her gaze stormy and a small muscle in his jaw began to tick with impatience.

"I have it on good authority that your life is in danger." He fought the churning undercurrents in his veins and kept his tone even. "I need you to smile like you've met a friend rather than the devil incarnate."

"No." Her mutinous glare told him hell would freeze over before she'd accompany him anywhere. "I have my own security arrangements. There's no need for your involvement."

Damn she was obstinate. He glanced at the bare skeletal trees that lined the empty street. "I don't see your security guy. Do you?"

"You're insane if you think I will smile and get in that car with you. For all I know, you could be the one who wants me dead."

"Trust me. I very much want you alive." That was an understatement. He wanted her naked and panting in his bed. He shook the provocative image from his head. That was hardly what Bob had in mind when he entrusted his precious princess to Nico's care.

"What does it matter to *you* if I'm alive or dead? You were less than interested if my memory serves me correctly." The choppy rush of her breath told him she hadn't forgiven him. That, and her bunched up fists.

"It matters to your father." He hoped she'd see sense and get into the vehicle of her own free will, so he didn't have to go through with the whole abduction scenario. Besides, she'd be just as likely to ignore the threat of a gun to her ribs. He could hardly fire the thing and his credibility would be blasted to Hades.

"What does my father have to do with this?"

"We don't have the luxury of time to stand here and discuss it. Please get in the car and I'll tell you the whole story." His internal thermostat roared into overdrive.

"Tell me first and then I might, *might*, get in the car with you." Her eyes bored into his and the Dr. Seuss story of the North-Going Zax and the South-Going Zax played out in his mind… they could well be standing foot to foot and face to face until the end of time.

"You're a key witness in a criminal trial. Without you, the perpetrators go free. With your testimony, they face many years in a Thai jail. Let me think, hmmm, *maybe* they might decide to silence you before you can incriminate them. Then they can get on with their lucrative work. You stand between them and freedom. Come on, princess, who do you think will come off second best?"

Abby stood still, her chest heaving and sweat beading on her face. Her heated scent near drove him to distraction. Standing this close to her soft curves and hard planes was a hell far from freezing!

He gave it one last try before he fully planned to use his superior strength to push her into the car whether she liked it or not.

"I have an obligation to keep you safe. *You* have an obligation to stay safe. If you won't come for your own protection, come because those felons deserve to be behind bars, not turning young children into sex slaves." He stormed over and threw open the passenger door, a wild pulse ticking in his throat, his gaze pinned to hers.

"How dare you question my integrity!" She stepped out of the stalemate and into the front seat of the car. He slammed the door and took a deep, steadying breath before striding around to the driver's side. His inner radar picked up a flash of movement out of the corner of his eye. Damn. Now, he just had to get her out of the country.

Who the hell did he think he was? Abby fumed as she sat in the plush leather seat, leaving sweat stains no doubt. Served him right. He was an insufferable man. Arrogant. She refused to look at him, preferring to look out of the tinted glass at the familiar surroundings.

"Sorry about your date." His eyes shifted to the rear-view mirror and back to the road.

"My date?" She was too astounded to stay silent.

"Your previous commitment. Remember?" His dark eyebrows lifted, and she couldn't stop the flush of heat to her cheeks.

The rat. He'd caught her out and couldn't resist a little gloating. Damn him to hell and back.

"I didn't say I had a date. I said I had plans." Plans that didn't include him or her father's machinations. "I have work tomorrow. I can't just disappear. How long do you plan to *hide* me?"

"Until the trial." His tone suggested he didn't want this job any more than she wanted him to whisk her away to safety.

"Don't worry. They've been notified of your absence."

"Just for the record, I think it's weak to run and hide from someone who threatens you." Or in her mother's case, to hide in the safety of her home, too afraid to leave.

Nico's chin lifted as he checked the mirror again.

"Princess, you come from the land of sugar plums. Have you never heard of the big, bad wolf? Where I come from, little red riding hood gets molested, gobbled up, and her bones spat out. What's worse, no one gives a damn beyond whether there's enough flesh left over to feed their family."

His words were crude and razor-sharp, and she felt their impact like a slap to her cheek.

"You don't like me very much, do you?" She'd tried hard to put his criticism behind her, yet the old wound festered still.

"I'd be surprised if you cared. Oh, I have a letter here from your father." He reached into his pocket and pulled out an envelope with her father's company's insignia on the front.

Abby took it and opened it. She recognised her father's handwriting and sighed with resignation as his words hit home. Staying safe would ensure these men went to trial and were put behind bars. But her insides clenched when she read his words of praise for the man sitting beside her—the only man her father would entrust with her life—and she had to wonder if her father had a secondary motive.

He adored Nico like a son, and it would be just like him to interfere in her love life.

Not that she trusted his judgement on that score any more than she trusted her own. She didn't need a man in her life, especially not one who'd made it more than clear she didn't come close to being good enough. Nor did she need Nico as her bodyguard. She was more than capable of employing her own. "Typically, my father thinks he knows what's best for me."

"Perhaps on this occasion, princess, he does." Nico glanced in the rear-view mirror and accelerated, pushing her back in her seat.

"Do you have to call me that?" She reached out to brace herself against the dashboard. She'd be lucky if she survived his crappy driving.

"It's what your father calls you."

"Exactly. You can call me Abby."

"Well, Abby, it looks like we're being followed. Chances are we have a problem." His gaze shifted back to the rear-view mirror, and his jaw set in a firm line.

"Are you serious?" She glanced behind them and saw a black SUV with tinted windows, angling into the space behind them.

"No, I thought I'd terrify you for the fun of it."

"It's probably my security detail. That's what I pay them for." The vehicle closed the short distance between them and rammed into their bumper. Abby grabbed hold of the seat and her stomach tangled itself into knots.

"I don't think so. Hold on."

Tension brought bile to the back of her throat and she held on tightly as Nico accelerated and wove through the traffic on City Road. He turned sharply into Montague Street, and accelerated briefly before hurtling into a car wash café. He pulled up behind the building and Abby held her breath and waited, her attention pinpointed on the access route behind them, her mouth dry. Her heart pounded like a fist to her chest.

"I don't think they saw us. Here." Nico handed her a black

motorcycle helmet and coverall. "Put these on. Quickly." He reached for a helmet himself and a leather jacket, then got out of the car and pulled them on. With the visor down, no one would recognise him through the darkened Perspex. He strode the short distance to a black Harley and her eyes widened. He couldn't be serious. She wasn't getting on that thing.

He straddled it and the motor blasted into life, sending a high-voltage jolt to her heart. She wriggled into the one-piece suit. She didn't have the first clue about motor bikes. She'd probably fall off. Nico banged the bike into gear and pulled up beside her.

He flicked the visor up, his blue eyes all edges and planes. "Get on, we need to go."

Adrenalin shot through Abby's veins, icy and sharp, and she couldn't move.

"Now."

His tone fired her temper and the freeze-frame in her limbs passed. How dare he speak to her like that? She swung her leg over the back of the bike and fought to maintain a dignified distance between herself and his broad, muscular back, but the minute he hit the throttle in warning, she leapt close. Her arms wrapped around his waist and her breasts pressed into his warmth. Her legs fitted snugly into the curve of his with an intimacy that brought a burning flush to her cheeks.

His leather-clad hand rested against her thigh.

Had he hoped to reassure her? Did he have any idea of the soul-shattering effect of his touch? She clenched her eyes closed, the fast acceleration making her hold ever tighter.

The wind shoved and pushed at them as they rocketed along the entry ramp and onto the freeway. The bike angled into a long, leaning curve and headed along CityLink towards the northern suburbs. She risked a glance over her shoulder. No sign of the black SUV. Thank goodness they'd lost them.

Her brain couldn't focus. Nico's hard leather-clad body protected her from the worst of the air-resistance, and the reassuring grip of his hand felt warm on her knee. Her pulse pounded, and her blood hit boiling point.

If this was his idea of safe, she'd hate to see danger.

Danger had been there. Right behind them. Not her security detail. So much for keeping her safe... unless, of course, Nico had paid them off? But someone had rammed them from behind. To force them off the road? It was an uncomfortable realisation that sent a chill through her fiery veins.

It was all she could do to stop the hysteria.

Nico would keep her safe.

As safe as she could be speeding at one hundred kilometres an hour on the back of a Harley Davidson. With Nico D'Antoni. And no clue as to where they were headed.

Chapter Three

The loud snarl of the motor stopped like its throat had been cut. Silence. Throbbing, noisy silence. Abby couldn't move. Her body refused.

Nico took off his helmet and after threading it onto the handlebars twisted around to look at her. "Are you okay?"

He helped her slide off the bike, his hands firm and solid around her waist. Her feet met the ground with a whimper, and it took a long moment before they seemed strong enough to take her weight. "No."

"You will be. It just takes a moment to get your land legs back."

Land legs? Ah, that's what was wrong. Her legs felt all spindly like an arachnid's, her bones as brittle as twigs. Her breath was jerky and shallow, and she fought to steady herself. She glanced around the undercover car park. They were alone—no sign of danger on the ramp behind them—and it looked like another vehicle change was on the cards. They'd pulled up beside a late model BMW sedan, silver in colour. She couldn't say she was sorry.

Nico reached over and lifted the helmet from her head, and she near fell into the fathomless blue of his eyes.

"Thank you." She donned polite aloofness to cover the crazy

wheeling of her pulse. "Who do you think…"

"You're welcome and I don't know for sure. Our intel was that your paedophile ring had links with an outlaw bikie group here in Melbourne. There were communications this morning that suggested the urgency of your protection was paramount."

He threaded her helmet onto the other handlebar and turned to unzip her coverall.

"I can undress myself." Her breath was jerky and shallow. He'd taken too many liberties in the past half hour and his disdainful opinion of her had been more than clear.

"I have another set of clothes for you." He swung his leg over the bike and reached into his pocket for a set of keys. He disengaged the lock, and the sound was like a gunshot to her nerves. Her rickety legs gave way and she grabbed at the bike to steady herself.

Nico reached into the boot and pulled out a shopping bag with a designer label logo on the side. "I took the liberty of selecting something in your size." His hand slid into his pocket and he pulled out a small ring box. "And you'll need these too."

Was he serious?

"We'll be travelling under the alias of Mr. and Mrs. Bortoli—honeymooners. Hence your need for wedding rings. New ones." He lifted the lid and an enormous diamond sparkled in the light, beside a plain wedding band.

"You're hiding *with* me?" Not for one moment had she interpreted 'go-into-hiding' as trapped-with-Nico-for-the-next-four-weeks! She'd thought he would hide her away in some remote place and get on with his busy life. She and Nico in the same space? He'd lost his mind. Honeymooners? What kind of sick joke was that? He'd rejected her 'puppy-love' outright and mocked her feelings—feelings she refused to feel

29

for him ever again. Love and weakness went hand in hand. "You bought me an engagement ring? A wedding ring?" He needed a straitjacket.

"An investment. Diamonds never depreciate." His tone was as crisp as the cold winter breeze that brought shivers to her skin.

Abby glanced down at the enormous rock he'd pushed towards her, the scent of his aftershave crowding her with memories of a kiss sought, stolen, and savoured. Musky, woodsy, spicy. As for the wedding band... He reached for her left hand and slipped the jewellery into place.

The rings felt heavy and foreign, but it was his touch—his warm, smooth touch—that sent her heart skittering in her chest. "What about you? Where's your golden shackle?" She held onto the bike like she was about to swoon. Why was he still holding her hand?

His eyebrow lifted and his forehead creased. "We're going to have to work on that attitude, Mrs. Bortoli." He held her gaze for a long moment, and complex emotions swirled in his eyes. "I haven't met too many women who share my view of matrimony."

"Then how ironic that we've ended up together in this sham of a marriage."

"But to the world, we're madly in love and can't get enough of each other. And there's champagne of course." He lifted the back of her hand to his lips and her breath jammed in her throat.

"Oh, bring on the champagne."

"We'll get to that, but for now, we need to get changed. And fast. Here." He handed her the shopping bag. "Do you want to get changed in the front or the back?"

"Behind the passenger door will do. There's no one around except for you, and you're too much of a gentleman to look." Her voice sounded hollow in the concrete layered space of the multilevel carpark.

"Do you think?" His tone was wry.

"You'd better be, or Mr. Bortoli might sport a black eye."

"There's nothing funny about marital abuse." He turned away and pulled off his leather jacket, his movement fierce.

"No, you're right." She reached into the bag and found a very tasteful black woollen dress, opaque black tights, and Italian-leather boots in the latest design. "You had some help with these I see."

"Yes, the saleswoman was very... helpful."

"She has expensive taste." Abby studied the soft leather.

"Fortunately, your father can afford it."

"Of course." She should have known her father was bankrolling this little escapade. "It's been quite a while since my father paid for my clothes." If she could get her body to coordinate, she'd make it to the car...

"You can't be serious."

"I pay my own way." His movements stopped mid-thrust into a woollen jacket. She could tell from his incredulous expression he didn't believe her. "My own rent. My own food. My own everything." And she didn't care what he thought of her. Not anymore. Well, maybe she did, or she wouldn't have felt the need to correct him.

"Very autonomous for the pampered daughter of a multi-billionaire."

"I gave that up." From the moment Nico had shared his scathing opinion of pampered daddy's princesses. He'd helped her to see the truth and he'd been right to criticise her. Not that she'd ever admit it to Mr. Perfect... ly Annoying.

"Why?" He settled the garment around his shoulders. His strong, round, muscular shoulders. His chest was... she swallowed. Delectable under his fine cotton shirt.

"Suffice to say it was my choice."

"A commendable one."

His approval warmed her from the inside out like a sweetened hot chocolate on a cold, blustery day. The blood returned to her limbs and she retreated to her side of the car. What she needed was a shower. Her running gear was damp, and as soon as she peeled away the thick insulation of the motorcycle suit, her body was racked with shivers. Her hands felt like lumps of ice, and getting into the dress, let alone the tights, was as challenging as a Mensa puzzle.

"Do you need help over there?" Nico appeared from the other side of the car, dressed and ready.

"No. Thank you. Where are we going and how long will it take?" Her teeth chattered and her skin puckered and tightened. "I'd give my right arm for a hot shower."

"We're headed somewhere safe, but I can have you showered and warm within the hour with no need for bodily sacrifices." He grinned.

"I might get to like you yet." The words were said in jest, but she was surprised to find she meant them.

Nico paced while he waited. Bob had entrusted his precious princess to Nico, and he would deliver her back to the man in one piece, with her modesty intact and her heart whole. He was there to protect her and keep her from harm. *Nothing more.* He liked his women fast and furious, with no strings attached. Abby was like Macramé—all fancy knots and entanglement.

A man would be a fool to think he could dally there and not come out scarred for life.

He opened the driver's door and lowered himself into the seat only to see Abby's rear end pointed towards him, toned and tantalising, her body sideways in the seat, her head lowered as she wriggled her foot into a boot.

His hands itched to follow the tempting curve of her spine. Her body was lithe and shapely, which was not how he remembered her at all. Back then she'd had curves, soft curves that spoke of over-indulgence, but these curves were more Grand Prix racetrack and just as deadly. Eyes off her beautiful tush. He had to keep his wits about him. They were far from out of danger, and he couldn't afford to drop his guard. The muscles in his abdomen knotted and pulled, and his fingers tapped a restless beat on the steering wheel. They had to move. Now.

"Come on, Abby. We need to go." Stress rose like liquid in his oesophagus... any higher and he'd drown.

"Almost done." Her words were breathless.

Nico refused to look in her direction. Getting dressed together spoke of an intimacy he'd shared with very few women—and in the past, it had always meant getting naked first.

Eyes front. That didn't stop his blood racing south for the image of her tush was etched into his brain. Nor the rapid volley of his pulse.

"Okay. All done. Let's go." She flung her bike gear into the back and turned to face him, confused. "I thought we were in a hurry."

Ninety-nine percent of his concentration was on fighting the appeal of her figure in that body-hugging dress, and he had to force his mind back from places more sticky than quicksand. "We do." He started the engine and manoeuvred the vehicle out of the small space.

"So, where are we headed?" She pulled the band from around her hair and regathered her ponytail, checking the mirror to rewind it.

"Do you still like to ski?" She was the pampered daughter of a billionaire and had travelled overseas every year of her life.

"I'm more of a snowboarding kind of gal now."

"You're a shredder?"

"You sound surprised. My father didn't mention that while the two of you were conspiring to abduct me?"

"You've changed. You're different from the Abby I used to know." And he couldn't afford to like who she'd become. "Your father wants me to keep you safe. You're lucky he cares."

His words were met with silence, which was a relief because she was a distraction, and he had a job to do. A job he was usually good at.

Nico turned into the public car park at the Essendon Fields airport and cut the engine. He strode around the front of the car to open Abby's door and scoped the area for anything suspicious. They were a newly married couple, and he should have eyes for nobody but his new wife, which suited him fine since he couldn't keep his eyes off her in that dress.

"I'll get our suitcases. I took the liberty of packing for you. It won't take long until we're off, and then you can have that shower you're longing for."

Damn. The image of her naked and streaming with water flashed into his mind. He reached for the luggage and lifted it out of the boot.

"I can take mine." The determined jut of her chin and her

straight back declared louder than words that she was far from the pampered miss she used to be.

This woman had backbone—a very appealing one—and she'd caught more than his attention, she'd caught his interest, and that was nothing short of dangerous in their current circumstances.

"Fine. Here." He pulled the handle out of the top of her suitcase and passed it to her. "I've got our passports." Organised by his contact at the witness protection unit.

He banged the boot and pressed the auto-lock. He'd drop the keys at the security desk and someone from D'Antoni would collect it, along with the bike and gear.

Extending the handle on his own suitcase, he fell into step beside her, and took her hand—her soft, silky hand—in his. He attributed the spike in his pulse to adrenalin and with his senses on hyperalert to anything suspicious around them, he didn't notice as her fingers curled against his like they belonged there.

Nico's possessive grip promised all kinds of magic. He strode beside her, all strength and muscle, on guard and bristling with defensive energy. It would take a brave person indeed, to snatch her away.

Abby found she liked it. A little too much.

She let his warmth seep into her bones, and she felt shielded and safe.

Which was just plain stupid considering she was being whisked away to avoid being killed… Someone had been right there. Right behind them. What if Nico hadn't forced her to go with him when he did? She shuddered and her bravado drained away.

Mr. Bortoli took care of every little detail and she let him, her thoughts in a spin. Fear was a tight throb in her veins and her head bobbed on her neck as she craned around to look behind her.

"We're clear. My staff have us covered." Nico took her hand and winked, and her body overheated.

"You can relax for the moment." He handed their luggage over for scanning and when the formalities were done, he placed his hand in the centre of her back and guided her out through the glass security doors onto the tarmac. His touch scorched through to her skin and when he pulled her close, his body shielding her from behind, her pulse thudded in her ears.

A ray of sunshine shone through the scudding clouds and drew her attention to the sleek, private jet that waited on the tarmac. A pilot and steward stood at the open door atop a short flight of stairs, dressed in navy-blue uniforms and aviator glasses.

The role of adoring new bride came shamefully easy, but when Nico lifted her into his arms to carry her up the stairs, her heart jammed in her chest. Her breath caught. Darn it. Get it together. "What are you doing?" she whispered, her words, ragged and torn.

"Doesn't a groom carry his new bride over the threshold?" Nico's steps slowed, and his gaze captured hers.

"I think that's into their marital boudoir." She couldn't stop the hysterical giggle. Five years ago, she'd have given her father's entire fortune to be carried by Nico D'Antoni. Deluded. That's what she'd been. In love. The anguished teenage variety that afflicted not only her heart, but her soul. In lust. Out of her mind with desire and the fanciful fiction that Nico was the only man for her.

When they got to the top of the stairs, the pilot and steward welcomed them onboard with a grin. Nico thanked them before letting Abby slide slowly and carefully—provocatively—down the very masculine contour of his body. He pressed his lips, velvety hard, against hers. Surprised, she didn't even fight him. Her mouth fell open and his tongue entered in a daring ambush, a sensual stroke against hers, and she found herself lulled into a honeyed lethargy. Her bones turned to liquid, and something hot and fiery streaked through her veins. His kiss was blistering, a wicked tasting, and what kind of devilry made her kiss him back?

It was Nico who came to his senses first and invited space between them.

Eyelids heavy, Abby opened her eyes to find Nico's intense, unfocused gaze fixed on the bruised flesh of her lips. Whoa. She struggled to rein in her roaring reaction. What the hell just happened?

Lunacy. She'd lost her mind. And definitely her strength. And even now, she relied on Nico to keep her upright.

He'd touched a pristine part of her that still believed in fairy tale princes, but the more cynical part of her, borne five years earlier, had banished those little girl wishes to where they belonged.

They had no place in the real world.

She gulped the cold winter air like she'd been deprived of oxygen, which explained her light-headedness and her need to pull the fragmented parts of herself back together.

Nico held her close like he sensed her shattered bewilderment or like he too, had been taken by surprise.

That was no ordinary kiss. Never had a man taken her

lips and taken her soul. Possessed her so completely that her defences crumbled like they didn't exist. She absorbed his strength, his warmth… and wrenched back control of her senses. "What the hell was that?"

He pushed her away from him, his eyes no longer dazed, but stormy and agitated. "That, Mrs. Bortoli, was a marital kiss."

"Then marital kisses should come with some kind of warning." She stepped out of his embrace and into the opulent interior of the private jet. Taking a deep gulp of the expensive air, she sank into a soft leather seat. Sheesh. The man knew how to kiss.

"Damn right they should."

He fell into the seat beside her and Abby's body swam with sensations she didn't want to feel. She was dizzy—sweaty—and he was close. Too darn close.

"Maybe we should avoid them in future." Oh, hell, was that her voice? He was supposed to protect her, not kiss the life out of her.

"No doubt about it." He sounded disagreeable like it was *she* who had done something wrong.

"*You* started it." She scowled and scooted away, creating distance between them. His body was too hard, too imposing, too…

"You didn't make it easy to finish."

She was glad to hear it, because if he hadn't pushed her away, she'd still be clinging to him… like a lovelorn teenager. No way could she let that happen again.

She'd worked too long and too hard to get him out of her heart, and with one kiss, he'd wormed his way back in. Not. Going. To. Happen. She would not put herself through the agony of wanting Nico again.

He lounged beside her—powerful, sexy, stormy—but it was his brooding eyes that pulled at her insides and left her... weak. Knowing her weakness was the first step to conquering it; and conquer it she would.

Chapter Four

Nico sat shell-shocked. He'd had to dig deep—deep—to find the strength to step away from that kiss. It had sucker punched him and left him senseless. Disoriented. He'd started the kiss a master and finished a blithering slave.

Enslavement to Abby Kercher was akin to jumping out of a plane without a parachute. He needed to keep his eyes on what was important: self-preservation and Abby's preservation.

Mr. Bortoli might kiss his new wife with gusto, but Nico didn't want any part of it… what had gone wrong was that *Nico* had kissed Abby. No, what had gone wrong was that Abby had kissed him back and left him ravaged like she'd devoured his bones.

If she had the same effect on Ruapehu, the sleeping beast would roar into life and their lives would be far from safe. When had it last erupted? Fifteen years ago. If there was the smallest spark of life left in it, they were in trouble.

The jet taxied down the runway and Nico tightened his seatbelt. Abby stiffened beside him as they lifted off the ground, and he reached for her hand. Hell. The slightest contact with the woman was a hazard. She created more tension in his body than a childhood thrashing.

They powered through the dark tempest of the clouds and found sunshine and the open sky above. The plane levelled out and the roar of the engine eased, along with the deranged thump of his pulse. The steward arrived with champagne and Nico waited while Abby's glass was filled and then his own. He held it up in mock salute. They had a role to play, and they would have to play it well if they were to stay safe.

"To you, Mrs. Bortoli, and a terrific honeymoon."

Her eyes—a bewitching green—widened and her pupils flared. "To you, Mr. Bortoli, and our new life together."

May we survive it.

She raised the glass to her lips, and he had to drag his gaze away. She left him witless and that wouldn't do. Not when he needed to keep her safe.

"If it's okay with you, I'd like to take that shower."

Her words arrowed into him, deep and barbed. "Sure," he croaked and grappled for air. "Your suitcase is in the bedroom."

"Bliss." She harpooned him with her eyes. "Thank you, Mr. Bortoli."

"You're welcome." Her smile was a radiant beam, and he couldn't draw a full breath until she stepped away and took her sweet and musky scent with her.

Where was the shallow miss he remembered from five years ago? The young socialite who'd been more interested in appearances than what was on the inside. Which suited him just fine because what was on *his* inside was black to her white. Besides, he liked his women mature enough to understand the difference between love and physical attraction, and sensible enough to know when a liaison had run its course.

He sipped his champagne and sat in melancholy silence.

Abby was forbidden fruit. That was why she'd gotten under his skin. And that kiss? That kiss had left him blind-sided.

That kiss had been fuelled by fear and the thrill of escape. He had nothing to worry about. He would regroup and get on with ensuring the rest of the trip went to plan.

"Did I say thank you already." Abby settled into the seat beside him, with a waft of spice and all things nice. "I love the clothes. I feel like a new woman. I am a new woman. I'm Mrs. Bortoli. This marriage thing could be fun."

Fun? Damned if he didn't feel the need to contradict her.

Fun kisses were his specialty and that kiss had been far from fun. Fun didn't make the earth shift on its axis. Fun didn't leave a man tied in knots. Fun didn't drive a man to the edge of crazy.

Yet here she was. Bright and bubbly and sipping her champagne like they were off on a grand adventure, like men married her and bought her underwear every day of the week.

The thought of her in the perky briefs he'd selected for her had him feeling like they'd flown too close to the sun. "We still have a few more hours in the air." The words corkscrewed up from somewhere tight and frustrated.

"Are we heading to New Zealand?"

She settled into the soft leather seat beside him, her gaze sharp. She'd brushed her hair into a fresh ponytail and his temperature spiked afresh. Thank God it was somewhere cold—all going well. The last thing he needed was for the mountain to erupt.

"Yes, Mount Ruapehu. On the North Island."

"Oh, I've heard of it, but I've never been there." Her brow creased and then she jerked forward, her body tense. "Wait, didn't that mountain erupt? It was on the news... you're taking

42

me to an active volcano… to keep me safe?"

"That was a long time ago. It's dormant now and more than safe." Although, there was a good chance the mountain would stir into life the moment she set foot on it, and with the ski field not five hundred metres from the volcanic crater perhaps his decision had been misguided. "There's no need to worry."

He could see from the expression on her face that she wasn't convinced. Fault lines crossed the earth. He doubted any place was safe from her kind of energy.

"I'm sure you wouldn't take me anywhere dangerous."

The steward interrupted with a selection of magazines and Abby chose a glossy women's magazine. Nico's heart lurched in his chest and banged against his ribs. He knew what lurked in there, and if he could have snatched it back from her without appearing rude, he would have. The melodrama was splashed across the front: 'Australia's Ten Most Eligible Bachelors'. The press hadn't done him any favours.

He hoped New Zealand was far enough from Australia. He hadn't counted on the article when he'd devised his honeymooning couple plan. But then, if anyone discovered his identity, they'd just think he was a celebrity seeking to protect his privacy.

Four weeks. He just had to keep her under wraps for four weeks. He reached for his champagne, and his usually brimming-with-solutions mind was silent. It gave him nothing. Nothing but the sound of his fast-beating heart. She might not see the article. And if she did, he'd just explain, and they'd move on.

She probably wouldn't be interested enough to read it. He should pre-empt it… "I probably should warn you," he began, but flailed around on the hook of her gaze. "I'm a traditionalist.

I prefer to ski." Coward.

The amusement in her eyes was intense. "I'll forgive you, Mr. Bortoli, but you should have disclosed that fact before we got married. I might not have gone through with the wedding."

"Secrets have a way of coming to the surface, don't they? Do *you* have any I should know about?" Hell, he didn't want to know her secrets. It was hard enough to keep his distance as it was.

"I *might* snore." She half-smothered the words behind her hand.

"*That* could be a deal-breaker." Nico couldn't imagine anything grotesque coming from the lush paradise of her mouth.

"Well, it's more like heavy breathing."

Some reassurance. That catapulted him into even more dangerous territory, making Mount Ruapehu and an untimely eruption seem benign.

"You might have to sleep alone."

The quick flash of panic in her eyes brought a chuckle to his throat. She hadn't thought that far ahead. Married couples slept together. Honeymooning couples shared a glamorous boudoir with a king-sized bed.

"Oh!" Her eyes widened.

"Don't worry. I won't banish you from our marital bed, not even if you snore like a gaggle of geese."

Now her face turned to horror and he all-out laughed.

"Tell me you're joking. You don't truly think we're going to share a bed?'

He checked that the steward was still out of ear shot. "Sharing a bed is the best way to keep you safe at all times."

Abby took a deep gulp of her champagne and choked when

it went down the wrong way. He patted her back and tried to help, but her face burned, and she grappled for breath. She fanned her face and when she settled back into her seat, she turned to him.

"Well, maybe we shouldn't. I wouldn't want to keep you awake. You need to be alert." He wasn't oblivious to the fresh wave of pink that coloured her cheeks.

She'd kept him awake for years or at least a hologram of her had but the woman who roused him from his sleep was a figment of his own imagination—like Abby in form, but very different in substance.

Sex dreams were the stuff of youth and at thirty-two years of age, he had no excuse beyond the fact that the woman beside him was as lethal as a designer drug. One taste, however miniscule, and a man's body craved more. Fortunately, his head was tougher than that. It took a very tough head and a no-prisoner's kind of will to get from where he came—to where he was now.

Abby's heart bounced around in her chest like a ping pong ball on steroids.

My God, he couldn't be serious?

Surely her father hadn't intended for Nico to share a bed with her! That was taking fatherly manipulation beyond extreme or maybe this part of the plan was the brainchild of the Adonis beside her.

He probably expected women to sacrifice themselves at his feet. She flicked the pages of the magazine with a sharp energy that swirled the dust motes visible in the bright beam of sunlight that arrowed in from the window and refracted off the brilliant-cut diamond on her left ring finger. Her attention flitted from headline to headline, unable to focus.

There were many things she'd do to put these felons behind bars but sharing a bed with Nico was not one of them.

That kiss had been warning enough. The greatest risk to her person came not in the form of those who wanted her dead, nor in the potential for natural calamity, but in the form of her so-called protector.

He did things to her body that no other man could.

There would be no bed-sharing. No kissing. No touching of any kind.

She needed to formulate some rules and as soon as they were behind closed doors, she would declare them loud and clear. The hot shower had helped to restore her wits, and she'd decided the best defence was to diminish that kiss into something surmountable. Nothing out of the ordinary. Nothing of consequence. Nothing more than a flirty peck. A meeting between lips. A slide of tongues.

Hell, stop right there. No kissing. No kiss-thinking.

It was like she'd conjured him up in picture form on the page—and it took a long moment for her addled brain to believe her eyes.

Nico. Looking as sexy and dangerous as a gladiator. All tanned skin and gorgeous chest, a hormone-stirring landscape of hills and valleys... and a single tattoo on his left pec of a black bird flying free. The image ignited the still-burning embers at her centre.

One of Sydney's most eligible bachelors.

Oh, please. She'd been rescued by a man-bimbo? Worse, an obviously less than discerning man-bimbo who'd made it clear she didn't come close to meeting his less-than-high expectations.

Well, she had her answer. That kiss had been high voltage because the man doing the kissing had had plenty of practice.

They couldn't have been more polar opposite. She lifted her eyes to find him watching her with the intensity of a mountain cat.

"You can't believe everything you read."

"Where there's smoke, there's fire." If he thought he could soften her with that scowl, he was way off the mark.

"Sensationalism sells magazines. They're more interested in what makes a compelling read than anything to do with the truth."

"You don't owe me an explanation, except why you think anyone would buy the Mr. and Mrs. Bortoli story when just one person has to read the latest issue of this magazine and our cover is blown."

She lifted her eyebrows for emphasis and enjoyed watching him squirm. Two could play at that game!

"We're a honeymooning couple. No one will expect us to surface from our room for more than a moment."

"You can't seriously expect us to stay inside a hotel room for the next four weeks?"

"We can get out on the slopes without anyone recognising us, but we won't eat in public places. Room service will have to suffice."

The arrival of the steward with an antipasto platter and more champagne interrupted their surreptitious jousting.

"Thank you." Abby smiled at the young man and focused her full attention on the food. She was starving and had been too distracted to notice.

She turned her attention back to the article and took great delight in his obvious discomfort while she took her time digesting the myriad of small facts they'd thought to include.

So, he was not only the CEO of D'Antoni security, but an entrepreneur with a host of other investments, and a savvy public speaker. Interesting. There was a photo of him in a charcoal suit, pristine white shirt, and striped tie, in action at a lectern. Behind him was a slide with stock price movements. He looked very confident and passionate.

Curiouser and curiouser.

"How much longer are you going to study that?" His voice was a growl and way too close to her ear for her liking.

She gave him a back-off-or-else kind of look and the wise man took the threat for the real one it was and invited some distance between them.

Not enough. Not nearly enough.

"It's not my life splashed in print for all to see." Abby waved the magazine in his direction.

"I can hardly sue them for printing information that's available to anyone should they do an internet search. Have you ever searched your own name? You might be surprised by what you find."

She could tell from his smug expression that he'd done just that. Terrific. She could only imagine the information he'd uncovered there. A new wave of heat rushed to her cheeks, and she turned her attention back to the page in front of her, eager to shield herself from his all-knowing gaze.

Those piercing blue eyes of his looked right into a person... could he see the part of her she tried to hide? The part that shared her mother's fear? She could only hope not. And she didn't need to read the gossip-mongering to know she'd be painted as a poor little rich girl, a victim of circumstance.

She was no victim. Not ever. In Bangkok, she'd stayed alive

by playing dead. Not her proudest moment, but she'd lived, and the others had died. Gary had thrown himself on top of her and she'd been covered in his blood. He'd saved her life and she'd stayed still, too afraid to move. It was a dirty secret she kept to herself. It sounded weak and pathetic. Almost as weak and pathetic as waking up in a cold sweat or finding herself whimpering in the corner of her bedroom, her arms over her head. There were bigger worries in the world. Worries that made her all-consuming rumination seem tiny, miniscule, and self-indulgent.

She'd learned the hard way that there was nothing admirable about her. Not much beyond her father's bank account.

Nico on the other hand was a self-made man if the facts outlined in front of her were correct.

And then it struck her. Nico would never know whether a woman loved *him* or the trinkets his money could buy. Not unless he dated the wealthy. She ran her eye over the long list of his recent conquests and could see she was right. Stunning blondes. Supermodels. Leggy and gorgeous. Women blessed with beauty *and* money.

She was happier flying under the radar in Melbourne.

Just another ordinary person. Doing ordinary things. She'd learned the importance of being her own person. And being known for what *she* achieved, rather than what her father had achieved.

Nico took the magazine out of her hands, and she looked up in surprise.

"Lunch is being served." Nico's tone was bemused, as if he'd known her mind had travelled to places far beyond the here and now.

Abby straightened the recliner lounge into a more upright

position. She needed to get herself together.

"That's a lot of women you've dated. Short attention span?"

"You can't believe everything you read." His eyes cut like a razor's edge, and she welcomed the lashing disapproval. She didn't care how many women he entertained... okay, she did. Irrational was her forte. God knows, she'd lived with it through all of her growing years. Her mother was the Queen of Irrational. The Queen of Fear. The Queen of Hide-Behind-Closed-Doors. Her mother's fear had grown into a fully-fledged agoraphobia.

Abby planned to fight. She was a fighter and if that wasn't quite true, then she aspired to be a fighter. Which brought her back to the man beside her and suddenly, she saw the attraction. It wasn't irrational at all. It was rational in capital letters.

He was someone she could admire. He lived by a moral code. He was a battle-scarred fighter.

Chapter Five

New Zealand had a beauty as rugged and devil-may-care as the man who sat beside her, his hands on the wheel of the fancy hire-car they'd collected at the Auckland airport.

The four hours—and still counting—car trip had passed largely in silence and even now he brooded beside her.

Abby didn't mind. In fact, she preferred to turn her attention to the rugged landscape, all glens and hills, gorges and steep angles, like it had been clawed by a giant prehistoric beast. And away from the muscular terrain of the man who sat too close beside her. The light was now in its last throes, along with her capacity to withstand the constant thrum of her body. Her pulse hadn't settled in hours. Not with Nico's muscular thigh right there. Her cheeks flushed as pink as the colour that pearled across the sky in the west. The mountain loomed ahead—finally, thank the heavens—rising from the desolate scenery like an ancient beast. It looked peaceful enough, but the thought of finding sleep on its restless flank was unfathomable.

How could she shut her eyes when the volcano might choose that moment to open hers? There was no greater wrath than a woman scorned. How scornful was it to climb a sleeping beast and shimmy down its snow-covered belly? To build accommodation on its breast?

She shook the whimsy from her head and focused on more practical issues.

"Which ski resort are we headed to?" Her voice shattered the restless quiet. From the signage, there were two in the direction they were headed. Turoa and Whakapapa.

"Whakapapa, spelt with a Wh, pronounced with an f." His tone was wry.

The potential for eruption she'd feared from the moment she'd learned they were to ride on an active volcano, had her squirming in her seat, and she fully blamed the man smouldering away beside her, the antithesis of dormant.

"That's an unfortunate name." Her voice squeaked like a poorly played violin.

"But a useful marketing ploy."

"I'm sure you're right." She pulled herself together. "The landscape is spectacular."

"Just wait until you see the view from the top of the mountain. You can see for aeons. The crater lake is about an hour's walk from the top of the ski-lift. It's hot and steamy and an incredible turquoise colour."

"Sounds amazing." Her insides pulled tight and knotted under her ribs. "Let's hope we don't disturb her."

"There's no need to worry. She's been here since the beginning of time, and the New Zealanders have learned to live with her despite her temperamental nature."

"Hmmm."

"As a skier—shredder—you'll soon see she's worth the risk. Besides, the Chateau Tongariro, where we're headed, has been there for generations, Circa 1929. She's a grand old dame.

There's no reason to think that will change during our short visit."

"I'm sure you're right." Abby's voice quavered, and she swallowed against the tension in her throat.

"I didn't have you pegged as the worrying type."

She didn't answer him directly, instead turning her attention back to the scenery. It was savagely beautiful and spoke of age-old mystery. The deep sapphire blue of twilight gradually bled over the rosy pinks and the silver white of the snow covered peak.

They were nearly there.

"What does Ruapehu mean?" There must be some ancient folklore about it. She loved that kind of thing and wished she had her laptop with her so she could investigate further. She'd come with nothing of her own.

"You may not want to know."

Her heart stilled in her chest. Why wouldn't she? "Try me." She steadied her gaze on the growing beast of a mountain. "Know thy enemy and all that."

"There are two definitions as far as I'm aware, both Maori in origin. The first is exploding pit. The second is booming crater."

Of course.

"And this was the first place you thought of when you needed to secret me away somewhere safe?" What did that say about him? "Have you never heard of the Bahamas? Tahiti looks nice?"

He grinned, and she found she liked it.

A lot.

His eyes shifted from the road to hers, and she had to stifle the urge to smile. He was a far from straightforward man. She got that. She sensed his disturbance, the complex currents that ran beneath his rugged exterior.

She feared there was a lot going on beneath that quiet mountain as well.

"I thought you liked adventure."

If only he knew. And then her promise to herself raised its ugly head. Her words and actions had to be as honest as possible or she'd never close the gap between her internal and external worlds. "You're wrong. I'm chicken-livered. A fear-freak. Adventure is my nemesis."

The car lost power as his foot stalled on the accelerator and he turned to look at her. "You can't be serious."

"Sorry to disappoint you."

"You're in witness protection. Your life's under threat because you didn't stay safe, you didn't soak up the sun and sip a cocktail, you got yourself caught up in some harebrained rescue mission. And that didn't end well for your new friends."

"I fell into it more by accident than by design. If I hadn't met Gary…" She squeezed her eyes shut. She was glad she'd met Gary and his group of mates. She was glad she'd helped them rescue those innocent children. They'd introduced her to Project Karma and now, her life was meaningful… and they were gone. The thought brought sweat to her brow.

"Your friends—you—poached the children those scumbags used to ply their trade."

"Their families—the people they should have been able to trust—sold them to those lowlifes against their will. What would you have done?"

"Most tourists turn a blind eye." He reached out and rested his hand on her leg. She jerked back in response to his touch.

"If you play with fire, princess, you get burned. Covering

your eyes won't make what you don't want to see go away. Those lowlifes will do everything in their power to stop you from testifying."

Her anger balled like a fist and knotted under her ribs, as heated as the magma below the snow-covered mountain that loomed ever closer. "What makes you so wise? I would have thought 'exploding pit' was a dead give-away."

"Tropical island paradise would have topped their list of likely hideouts for a pampered princess."

"If you think that, then you don't know me. You never did." She pushed his hand away.

"Well, for better or worse, we have four weeks to get to know each other."

"If we survive it." Her tone was scathing. If the mountain didn't kill her—if they weren't discovered—Nico D'Antoni surely would.

Nico forced himself to bite back the words that slammed into his pressed lips, sharp and lethal. Words that would make the situation worse.

Abby sat with her head turned away from him, her body rigid.

She was the most infuriating, ungrateful miss he'd ever had the misfortune of being forced to spend time with. If she didn't care whether she lived or died, why the hell should he? She had less sense than the bugs splattered on the windscreen.

Darkness crept in on silent feet and the light of the moon appeared tremulous and timid. The beam of the headlights created an eerie tunnel through the gnarly black scenery and the white lines at the centre of the road shot towards him like arrows. Hell. He'd had no right to say what he'd said.

Fatigue washed over him, and he relaxed his vigilance just a little. There was no sign of anyone following them. Nothing to suggest they were in danger. Their destination was something he'd kept to himself. No one would know where they were holed up. They would be out of touch with the rest of the world.

The tension in his shoulders eased, and he realised Abby *did* care whether she lived or died, or she wouldn't have come.

Maybe that was what had ignited his anger. Why the hell had she ventured out of her diamond-encrusted existence, and risked life and limb to do the right thing when it didn't fit with what he knew about her? Who the hell was this woman and where was the far-from-endearing young miss he'd known? This version was dynamite dangerous to his peace of mind.

The chateau appeared out of the darkness, its windows throwing yellowed warmth across the crisp blue shadows. It was four levels of neo-Georgian mansion and the silent mountain rose steep behind it. Abby wouldn't be disappointed with their accommodation, even if she was disappointed with him.

The thought stabbed him somewhere deep and primitive.

He didn't give a fig what she thought of him. He didn't need her approval. He didn't need her thanks. He just had to keep his promise to Bob and deliver her home safely after the trial in Bangkok.

Pulling up in the car park, he cut the engine without preamble. Hunger dragged at his focus, and fatigue pulled at his limbs.

"Nico, I'm sorry."

An apology from little Miss Contrary?

"Apology accepted." Silence stretched between them. "I may

owe you an apology, too."

"If that was an apology, thank you." Abby bent forward to get a better view of the chateau. "This place is beautiful. I may have misjudged you. I can see the appeal."

"Let's agree to withhold judgement until we've spent more than a day in each other's company."

"That sounds fair."

He opened the door and stepped out into the biting cold. He reached into the back seat for the warm jackets he'd brought in anticipation of the crisp night air.

"Here, you'll need this."

Abby's cat-eyes held his in the half-light. "Thank you, you've thought of everything."

Was that humble pie on her whiskers?

The chuckle started deep in his gut and took him by surprise. No woman had ever more effectively brought him back from the depths of his temper. "Come on, let's get into the warmth."

Dragging their suitcases across the frosty glitter that coated the road, they slipped and slid toward the dramatic columns of the grand entrance portico.

The reception was opulent, and a massive chandelier illuminated the space with a thousand starry lights. Abby's gaze bee-lined to an instrument on the desk, and he couldn't stop the grin. At least the drama of the mountain would take her mind off the dangers of retribution. He'd have to make sure it didn't do the same for him. He needed to be on his guard.

"It's a seismograph," he whispered, close to her ear, and fast regretted his proximity when her head spun around too quickly for him to step away and their lips brushed, sending his pulse skyrocketing.

"Mr. and Mrs. Bortoli?"

It was like a magnetic force-field held him trapped. Her lips were the colour of passion, ripe and exotic like pomegranate. He fought the urge to taste and devour and tamped down that part of him that wanted to take her in his arms with no apology... steely determination strengthened his bones like an army arriving late to the scene of a battle and he stepped away, breaking the invisible entanglement.

Macramé. This woman came with more strings than a marionette, and he was no woman's puppet.

With check-in done, he led the way through an elegant sitting area. A huge fire burned under an exquisite mantle. Potted palms and heavy crimson curtains created private nooks with beautifully upholstered old chairs. He scanned the space—couples sat by the fire, relaxed, their attention on those nearest to them. Four teenagers played pool at the full-sized table. The chateau was meticulously maintained. He'd be surprised if Abby didn't find it to her liking. History abounded in every corner.

He pressed the lift button—the Te Heu Heu Suite was on the top floor of the Tongariro wing. The bed was a super king and would be quite expansive... large enough for them both to keep their distance. And whether Abby liked it or not—whether *he* liked it or not—that was the best way to keep her safe. What he hadn't figured on was the energy that sparked between them like an electric current.

They rode the lift in silence, both tired after their long trip.

Nico slipped the key card into the lock and pushed the door open. The suite was inviting and comfortable with a sensual ambience. Chandeliers gave the space a soft glow and a fire flamed in the hearth, clean heat from gas rather than wood. It was meticulous, spacious, luxurious, and welcoming with classic furnishings: a lounge in cream and gold, polished timber, rich heavy drapes, and plush carpet. Opulent. Elegant. And hopefully up to Abby Kercher's standards.

He waited while she ventured through the lounge room and into the bedroom. She'd like the marble ensuite... but there was only one generous sized bed, albeit barely visible under a mountain of cushions. What was it about high-end accommodation and cushions?

Abby poked her head back through the doorway. "Just what kind of adventure did you have in mind when you booked this?" Her gaze slammed into him.

"Not the kind *your* mind is entertaining. The bed is more than big enough to share without encroaching on each other's space. We can use those cushions to create something akin to the Great Wall of China down the middle of the bed. I think we're both mature enough to manage this situation without the need for hysterics. I need to be with you at all times, except when you're in the bathroom."

Abby stood like a sentinel for a full five minutes, her teeth bruising the flesh of her lower lip. "I'm not in the habit of sharing my personal space with a man. Nor of sharing a bed, no matter the size of the dividing wall." She took a deep breath and her jaw tightened. "I know that's probably incomprehensible to a bachelor playboy such as yourself, but it's not an arrangement I feel comfortable with."

"We're not sharing sexual favours, Abby. Just space." Macramé.

"No, I won't." She flushed beet red. "I'll get my own room and..."

"Mr. and Mrs. Bortoli are on their honeymoon." His teeth practically gnashed together. Was there no end to her precious naivety?

"Well, maybe we've just had our first fight and can't stand the sight of each other." She glared at him.

"I need to be with you at all times to keep you safe." He kept the volume of his voice low and soothing. "I can't guard you from a distance."

"From the frying pan into the fire."

"Trust me, I have your best interests at heart. Your virtue is safe with me. You're not my type."

Her eyes held his and tension pulsed between them. "Yes, you made that perfectly clear five years ago." Her tone was scathing. "But if magazines are to be believed, your type is any woman with a pulse."

"You're confusing *me* with the fiction in that magazine."

He admired the way she lifted her chin and stared him down as if *she* were the injured party.

"And you're confusing me with someone who *wants* to share your bed."

"I like my women experienced and mature enough to handle a casual relationship. I'm figuring you don't fit that definition."

"You say that as if it's a bad thing."

"Hell, no. It's a good thing. The last thing we need is complication."

"I'm figuring any form of commitment would be a complication for you." The sneer in her tone was more than his ego could handle.

"I told you not to believe everything you read." He strode towards her and ignoring the warning bells chiming in his head, he took her mouth with his and savoured her helpless surrender. Whether she liked it or not, he knew attraction when he saw it and what simmered between them was far from uncomplicated.

The kiss drew them into dangerous territory.

It was Abby who stepped back and broke the intoxicating spell. "Don't do that again." She shook with the effort it took her to hold herself together. It had been a long day and she looked done in.

"I'm sorry, but whatever attraction there is between us, it's mutual. If you dislike my kind of man so much, don't load your eyes with sexual innuendo, and I'll be more than happy to keep my hands to myself."

"You're wrong if that's what you thought you saw."

"A woman doesn't look at a man like that unless she wants him naked. You may not have had a lot of experience with the translation, but I have."

"You're deluded. The only hunger you see in my eyes is the type that comes from an empty stomach. We haven't eaten in ages." She lifted her chin, smug triumph in her eyes. "Is there a room service menu anywhere?"

"Over there on the table." Nico nodded towards it and allowed her to change the subject. But it didn't stop the thud of his heart or the hard reaction of his body.

Abby moved towards the menu, making a great show of avoiding him, but in truth her heart rattled inside her chest and her body felt shaky like she'd overdone her weights at the gym. She ran her gaze over the selections, the words swimming and leaping around on the page, and passed it to Nico, who made a quick perusal and reached for the phone. With a lift of his brows, he waited while she gave him her order. He repeated the information into the phone casually without taking his eyes from hers. Abby felt the intensity of his gaze like a caress.

61

A caress that lifted her skin follicles and turned her blood to jelly. She moved towards the floor-to-ceiling windows and looked out into the darkness. Her reflection spoke of studied concentration... in truth, she fought her unwanted longings.

She had less than no interest in Nico. Once bitten... besides his money didn't impress her, nor did his interest in casual affairs.

He was welcome to sow his seed as far and wide as he liked, so long as he kept his virulence away from her. Besides, her sexual encounters to date had been less than satisfactory. Not that she'd ever tell him that. She couldn't help but compare every potential lover with her teenage fantasy of Nico, and... no man could live up to the ideal. That explained why she couldn't... and since Gary, well, the trauma of her ordeal had made it worse.

Except when Nico kissed her, there was fire in her veins and it charged, hot and liquid, around her body like an electric current. She still felt frazzled. Breathless. Choked.

Sharing a bed with Nico was an unfortunate necessity—she appreciated the need to stay safe, and she needed to keep her mind on the main game. Four weeks of close proximity with Nico D'Antoni was a small price to pay to put those monsters behind bars. Her evidence was important, and Nico was right... murder in cold blood was their daily bread. Maybe retreat was necessary. And Nico had made the security guy she'd hired look like a kid in dress-ups, but it wasn't like she could afford the likes of D'Antoni Security.

As for Nico, and that hunger he'd so aptly recognised—was there no end to his talents—she was more than capable of protecting her personal boundaries. And maybe with Nico there, she'd finally get some sleep without the nightmares and cold sweats... or not.

Abby's skin crawled with awkward. She wrapped her arms around herself as if to physically hold herself together and stared out into the night. Stars stretched for a trillion miles and a bright moon hung heavy and voluminous in the sky, its light weaving through the trees to create long eerie shadows across the snow. Nico came up behind her, and the gravelly timbre of his voice lifted the fine hairs on her skin and stole her breath.

"That one is Mt Tongariro and the other one is Mt Ngauruhoe."

Abby tried to focus on the volcanic cones she could see rising from the plateau like fists fracturing the earth, their snowy peaks illuminated by the moon... and not on Nico's musky male scent.

There was a knock on the door, and she jerked, her heart pounding in her chest, her breath coming hard and fast.

"It's okay, Abby." He spoke like he might to a spooked horse. "That'll be our suitcases." He moved away to open the door, his voice muted as he thanked the hotel staff and collected their suitcases. He wheeled them into the vast walk-in robe off the bedroom.

Abby took a deep, long breath, grateful for the space between them. The suite was huge, but not large enough to stop the gut-stirring sensation of being overcrowded.

"Why don't you have a bath while we're waiting for dinner? It might help to relieve some of your fatigue. We've had a big day."

A behemoth of a day.

"Did you pack night wear for me?" Her face burned with the thought that he might have considered it unnecessary. It had been a long time since anyone had packed for her and it spoke of a level of intimacy…

"I did."

"Toothbrush, toothpaste, dental floss?"

"Check, check, check… along with make-up, make-up remover, deodorant, shampoo, conditioner…" He ticked off his fingers.

"You bought me underwear." Her tone was accusatory, and he flashed a grin.

"You would have suspected my motives if I hadn't."

She suspected his motives, period.

He didn't even like her. She'd gotten that message loud and clear, somewhere between pampered and princess. Why he factored on her Richter scale at all was lunacy—or old news.

The thought of a long hot bath played in her mind but getting naked with a flimsy wall between them seemed like a giant risk.

"I'll run that bath for you. There should be bubbles." His voice trailed off as he ventured into the adjoining room and was lost in the sound of the water that poured from the tap.

Abby went to unpack and was impressed by his choices. She didn't want for anything, not even flannelette pyjamas. How could he have known she liked to feel warm?

She see-sawed between despising him and feeling grateful.

He'd run her a bath. He'd bought her clothes. He'd found a place where hopefully no one would find her. She felt ridiculously cosseted and emotion snaked into her throat.

Standing alone was not an easy road but with Nico beside her, she felt more confident she'd make it to the trial alive. Alive, but at what cost to her heart?

Chapter Six

With her skin still zinging from the bath, Abby climbed into her warm, fleecy pyjamas and brushed out her hair. No make-up. Nothing to mask the real Abby from the man who waited outside.

Their dinner would be here shortly, and she wanted to make sure Nico had time for a shower, too. He must be exhausted. He'd done all the driving and the event hadn't finished until late the night before.

She pressed her ear to the door but could hear nothing beyond the piano music that played through the sound system. Maybe he'd gone for a walk? She pulled the door open and stepped into their bedroom. Her feet sank into the soft carpet.

Nico was stretched out on the bed, his breathing slow and steady. Asleep?

She tiptoed closer.

His face was softer in repose, his gritty determination less evident. Abby found herself fascinated by the lush row of black lashes that fanned his cheek. His jaw was peppered with sexy stubble that made her hands itch with the need to touch. He had the air of a lion resting in the sun, all powerful muscle and sinew at risk of lurching into ferocious life at any moment.

Abby held her breath, afraid to disturb him, but mesmerised

by his masculine presence. Nico was right. She'd been more than aware of the undercurrents that seemed to surge and wane, pulling her towards him and then pushing her away. She'd thought her attraction had died a humiliating and agonising death. Apparently, not.

He didn't do commitment—why should that put her off? He liked women. He liked sex. She'd wanted him for as long as she could remember. She wasn't looking for a husband. She just wanted to get him out of her head and out of her system so she could have a normal relationship instead of comparing every man she dated with a hot fantasy that probably wasn't even real. There was no reason why sex with Nico would be any better than sex with any other man; and at least she'd be able to get on with her life. Put her longing to rest.

He liked women.

She was a woman. She had a pulse—a fast-skipping, erratic, crazy pulse that seemed to speed up whenever his blue eyes centred on any part of her body. They had to share a bed anyway. Kill two birds with one stone. Resolve this thing once and for all. Face her fears. Stop running away from them.

What if she froze up and her body shut him out, too? She'd have to face him every day for the next four weeks and feel that awful sense of failure that had shattered her relationship with Gary.

She fought the rush of panic and forced her thoughts back to the article. It had been all speculation. There wasn't a single quote from Nico to confirm any of it, and he'd warned her not to believe everything she'd read. Was it possible for a man like him to have integrity?

It wasn't like she could avoid him. He was sharing her room, her bed, her personal space. She assessed the sensations shimmying through her as she scanned his killer-body. She'd promised herself she would face her fears in a staggered way. Starting with the lesser fears and working her way towards the more mountainous ones. And this had to be her Everest.

If she didn't do this, she could regret it for the rest of her life. Or become a social cripple like her mother.

No. She had more strength than that. She had to have.

It wasn't like Nico would want anything from her, beyond physical satisfaction.

Her gaze steadied on that part of his body that intrigued her most and heat rushed to her cheeks as she realised, he was hard inside his black jeans. An erection in his sleep?

Her insides tensed up. It would never work. She closed her eyes tight against the rush of emotion, a sob catching in her throat.

"What is it?" Nico's voice was gravelly with sleep. Her eyes snapped open and her gaze was ensnared by the cerulean blue of his.

"Nothing." The word rode on the wave of another sob. She forced herself to swallow. "I'm sorry I woke you. I thought you might like a shower."

"Abby, it's okay. We'll get through this. You're not alone. I have my tech people working on it and the folk at the witness-protection unit. If there's any intel of any kind, I'll know about it. We're safe here."

His kindness was harder to bear than his scorn.

"I'm fine. Thank you." She swallowed the unpalatable weakness. "I know we'll get through this. I know how thorough you are. I do feel safe."

She did? How could she not? He was muscle-bound and fierce yet caring and kind. She'd never felt more safe. Or more at risk. The hotel had a damn seismograph on the reception desk for goodness sake. But it was Nico who presented the biggest threat.

The woman was as transparent as the sea on a still day. Something troubled her. Something big, and Nico sensed it was more complex than anything he wanted to know about. He didn't do complicated. He had enough complications in his own life, without taking on anyone else's.

Besides, she had no reason for hardship beyond what she'd created for herself. She'd grown up on easy street her whole damn life. Well, except for... he didn't often think of the incident that had brought Bob into his life. So, she'd glimpsed the dark side of life—the side he knew like the back of his hand. She'd survived it and settled back into her bejewelled existence as the only child of one of Sydney's wealthiest men.

Except now she lived in Melbourne and worked in Melbourne and had created a life for herself away from her father's lavish lifestyle. And she'd survived an awful trauma.

He observed her surreptitiously as she settled into the window seat, her arms curled around her legs, her gaze on the night sky.

Her vulnerability dragged at him, pulling invisible strings that left him restless. With a shake of his head, he found some track pants and a t-shirt and headed for the shower. He didn't do pyjamas. Never had. Never would. But in the presence of royalty, one didn't display one's wares.

Cold water. He welcomed it. Maybe she was right. Perhaps any woman with a pulse was enough to excite him. Guilty as charged. There was nothing about Abby Kercher that could possibly appeal to him, yet here he was, salivating!

He'd just left the bathroom, rubbing his wet hair with a towel, when there was a knock on the door. Adrenalin shot into his veins and his muscles tensed. The men who wanted Abby dead had a lot to lose. He resisted the urge to reach for his weapon, instead twisting the towel into a wet rope.

He looked through the peephole and relaxed his grip... a waiter with their meals, each covered by a silver cloche. He pulled the door open and the fellow entered, dressed in a black suit and white shirt. He set up their meals on the polished timber table with elegant silver cutlery and fine bone china. A bottle of wine rested in an ice-bucket with two fine crystal glasses. He wished them both an enjoyable meal and the door whispered closed behind him, a puff of air from the passageway blowing cold against the fine sheen of sweat that plastered Nico's forehead.

"You must be hungry." Abby's words were nervous. The atmosphere in the room had been razor sharp since he'd stepped out of the bathroom, and his pulse thudded.

Her eyes raked over him, jade with lust, her attraction raw and intense. Hell. How had he thought this could work? Appetites of a different kind clamoured for his attention. Devilry danced in his head. Sin whispered in his ears.

"You're right, I am. Let's eat. I'm famished."

The air swirled with magic, and he forced his eyes onto the still-sizzling steak before him. It wasn't like Mr. Bortoli could go downstairs and trawl the bar for the kind of woman Nico needed to ease the craziness that stormed in his body. There was no relief to be had, and he would just have to get used to it.

Abby wasn't his kind of woman. She was the type who demanded a man's soul for services rendered. She would want it all, and her daddy would expect a ring on her finger... or his head in a noose.

"I have a proposition for you."

Oh, he didn't like the sound of that. He picked up his steak knife and sawed into the juicy eye fillet. "I didn't take you for the propositioning kind of woman." He couldn't keep the sexual innuendo from his words. Hell, it filled his head. He slathered his meat with the red wine and mushroom jus and tasted, the flavour exploding on his tongue. He chewed without taking his eyes from hers and washed it down with a gulp of wine as if the liquid could quench the fire in his veins.

"I'm not, which is why this is awkward." Her eyes dropped to the grilled snapper on her plate, and she picked up her fork.

Awkward? That's what this was?

He forced a chill into his tone... a shield between them. "Perhaps it should wait until tomorrow when we're not so deliriously tired. I'm not much good to you right now." To put it mildly. His thoughts bordered on madness.

"Perhaps you're right." She lifted her fork to her mouth.

Every sound in the room was amplified, like his senses were on hyperalert. And now he felt like a cad. "I'm sorry. I had the feeling I wasn't going to like what you wanted to say, but I can handle it. Fire away."

Words from a crazy man.

Her gaze swept over him, and he was back in the firing line without a doubt. He fully regretted every step of the journey that had gotten him to this moment, with this woman, in this room. He waited—his insides clenched in anticipation.

Her expression was masked as she lowered her fork and stated matter-of-factly, "I think we should have sex."

Her words sucked the oxygen from the air. "No. That's not

going to happen." Over his dead body. Where appetites had ignited, ashes remained. "Your father would never forgive me. *I* would never forgive me. You're in a vulnerable place. You need to feel safe. I'm here to help you, not to take advantage of the situation. No."

Her eyes remained fixed on his, but the she-devil in them had lost her attitude, leaving behind a crushed and vulnerable young woman who'd survived a heinous crime.

Damn.

She torpedoed through his defences like they were made of custard rather than years of careful construction.

"This is not about whether I find you attractive. It never was. It's about the fact that I'm employed to protect you and I take that responsibility very seriously. Besides, I'm not the right man for you." His words were artless, but he'd lost the finesse required to soften their edges. He settled back into his chair and reached for his wine.

"I'm not asking you to marry me." Abby's eyes glistened. If she had the smallest inkling of what she did to him with a single glance, they'd be in big trouble.

"We have to share a bed anyway. It would save you from constructing the Great Wall, but if the idea is distasteful to you, then I apologise. I shouldn't have mentioned it."

No, she shouldn't have mentioned it, because now, he could think of nothing else. "Abby, I promised your father I would look after you and keep you safe."

"My father would protect me from the air I breathe if he had half the chance and look how that turned out for my mother." She lifted her glass and took a sip of wine.

"What do you mean?"

"My mother's a very private person." Abby appeared to

oscillate between the need to confide in him and the need to protect her mother's privacy. Hell, if she didn't trust him yet, she never would.

"My mother suffers from anxiety. Crippling anxiety. She's too afraid to leave the house. My father mollycoddles her and protects her from any situation that might lead to an anxiety attack."

Nico's body froze and his skin felt like it had been stung by a thousand fire ants. Raffaele had ruined the poor woman's life—how had Nico not known the extent of her trauma? How could Bob have been so kind and supportive of him when his wife suffered so terribly? Nico eyed Abby across the table and his promise to Bob sat uncomfortably between them. "Has she sought professional help?"

"She tried but it didn't work out. She's fine when she's at home."

Nico cut his steak with feigned nonchalance as if his insides didn't heave and shift with the force of the blood rushing through his veins. She'd put a ticking time bomb between them, and he tiptoed around the thing, unsure how to deal with it. "Is that why you moved to Melbourne?"

"I needed to prove to myself..." She paused and shifted her glass on the table. "...that I could be my own person and survive outside of my father's very sizeable shadow." Tears welled in her eyes and it took every fibre of his being not to step around the table and take her in his arms. "I don't want to be like my mother."

"You're fighting for what you believe in. You put your own life at risk to save others. If that's not courage, then I don't know what is." He was surprised to find he believed it.

"I have to fight my fear every day." She toyed with her cutlery.

So, she hadn't come out unscathed either. He understood better now why she'd chosen to testify, and he would keep her safe if it killed him—saying no to her very appealing offer nearly had. Sex with Abby, no strings attached? No need for the great dividing wall?

But he'd promised to protect her, and unlike his brother, he had a moral code. It sounded like Abby suffered from symptoms of post-traumatic stress… which made it even more imperative that he protect her. He'd promised her a wall and a wall she would get. A mighty big dividing wall that would keep them both safe and sane.

She claimed she wanted his body, not marriage, but what stormed between them was deeper and more provocative. It would take a brave man to venture into that Aladdin's cave. Or a crazy one. And therein lay the problem. She drove him to madness.

There.

The cushions were piled high, complemented by anything else he could find to keep her distant.

He pulled the doona up to his chin and lay still, his body swarming with sensations, his breath jerky and uneven, jagged in the silence. Hell, she'd know he wasn't asleep. He knew she wasn't. "Abby, are you awake?"

"No." Her voice was muffled. "I'm asleep."

He chuckled and to his discredit, he found he wanted to dismantle the damn wall and give her what she wanted. What they *both* wanted.

"Why do you want to have sex with me?" His tone was caramel smooth belying the ratcheting intake of his breath. "I told you years ago to keep yourself for someone worthy of you."

"You are worthy."

That sent his pulse into orbit. Damn the woman. He'd thought her answer might help put the thought to rest, because until he knew why she'd asked him, he would never get to sleep.

"You couldn't possibly know that."

"I wouldn't have married you otherwise."

Hah. "That's hardly an accolade."

"It's the best I've got right now. Give us another day together and I'll work on the specifics." Her voice was a soft vibration, muffled as if she'd burrowed into the warmth of the bed cover.

"We'd better get some sleep." He needed his wits about him, but she sent them into a spin. He couldn't afford to be off his game.

"You haven't changed your mind?"

"No, absolutely not. The wall stays."

"That's probably for the best. I decided it was too hot for pyjamas."

The little minx! The last thing he needed was an image of her naked and within touching distance. Damn provocative, wicked wench.

He could hear his own father's roar of laughter. Laws are made to be broken, son. It's hardly a sin if the woman's consenting. Not that his father knew the first meaning of the word integrity. It had taken Nico years to realise his father's precious crop in their back garden was marijuana.

He closed his eyes and rolled away from the temptation on the other side of the bed, trying hard to focus on his plan to keep her safe. He had a battalion of staff on the job. He'd know the minute a potential suspect stepped a foot in their direction and five of his men were in Bangkok keeping an ear to the ground. Really, he should relax. He hadn't had a holiday in so long he couldn't remember.

He didn't feel relaxed… in fact he'd never felt so strung-out.

His body was achingly awake, and Abby's every breath caught his attention. It was a while before her breathing steadied and became more regular. His own eyes remained open and fixed on the red numbers of the digital clock beside the bed. They mocked him for the lunacy of his decision as they flipped through to the wee hours of the morning. They were both consenting adults. Her choices had nothing to do with her father, and her father would never know.

But Nico would know and therein lay the problem.

Chapter Seven

Raffaele paid cash for his cabin at the Rotorua Thermal Holiday Park. The place stank like rotten egg from the local hot springs and steaming mud that were high in sulphur. He dropped his bags on the threadbare carpet and pulled the garish curtains aside. Not far away his brother was holed up with his whore. Raffaele's temper steamed as hot as the earth. He'd had them in his sights for a full ten minutes before he'd lost them, but he'd retraced his steps and found their car abandoned. Easy enough to wait and see who picked it up... and follow them. Four blokes from D'Antoni. They'd finally led him to Essendon Fields Airport after dropping staff at multiple sites along the way. His brother was savvy, he'd give him that.

Raffaele moved into the small kitchenette and reached for the plastic kettle. The tap shrieked as he turned the faucet to fill it, but the water looked clean enough. He flicked the switch and eyed the small collection of teabags.

He wasn't sure what annoyed him most. The flash private jet they'd travelled in or their fancy accommodation at Mount Ruapehu. No yellow and black label teabags there he'd wager. He surveyed the mugs and reached for the least chipped and coffee stained.

He'd had a break with the hire car. Hacking into their computer system had been easy enough, but he'd lost precious days to the task despite only two rentals fitting the time frame. Not to mention the tedious work required to scour the local CCTV footage to work out where they had headed.

But now he was here. He reached into his bag and pulled out the second-hand laptop he'd bought before he left Melbourne. He punched in the free Wi-Fi code and searched D'Antoni Security Services. He settled his gaze on the prissy photo of his brother, CEO... and his blood boiled as furiously as the water in the kettle. Shouldn't the bloody thing turn itself off? He eyed the blast of steam and got up to flick the switch.

It would be no hardship to kill Dominico and after the song and dance his brother had led him on, Raffaele was more than a little pissed-off.

He poured the scalding water into the mug and jiggled the teabag, sloshing liquid onto the faded laminate counter. He'd enjoyed killing Lorenzo. His former friend had taken his last breath with fear in his eyes. That's right. His horny behaviour had stymied any chance Raffaele might have had of a lighter sentence. He would have enjoyed castrating the dog—but he wasn't going back in the slammer for anyone. More believable that Lorenzo binged on booze and drugs and misjudged the mix.

Tomorrow, Raffaele would visit the Chateau Tongariro Hotel. Even the name was fancy. Dominico was predictable to a point. Raffaele sipped his tea and pondered the best way to kill them. Food poisoning? Exposure to the elements. They could get lost on the mountains and suffer an injury. He had time. Time to work out what was best... something painful and prolonged for his brother. Something swift and served cold for his whore. Raffaele flicked to the Project Karma Facebook page. The broad was a do-gooder like his brother, and heads had rolled, literally, when Bruno had learned she was alive. That doco had been illuminating...

With only a couple of weeks until the trial and no sign of trouble, he figured Dominico would be off his guard, although how anyone could feel safe on an active volcano was beyond rational. If only there was a way to force the mountain to erupt.

Raffaele had always known he was smarter than his dumb arse dobber-brother. Dominico's millions didn't make him smart—sure, he was lousy rich with a drum rolling emphasis on lousy. Lousy traitor. Lousy lip-flapping eavesdropper. Lousy brother who'd got lucky while Raffaele had rotted in prison.

Maybe he should cut the line on their brakes? No. He couldn't risk either one of them surviving the accident, especially not the whore. Or *his* head would roll. Besides, they might not use their car until they were on their way back to the airport for the trial. It was too risky. Her death was his stay-alive-in-jail card—his stay-alive-on-the-outside card—his stay-alive card.

He got changed and readied himself for a run. First, a hundred push ups, biceps then triceps. A hundred squats and lunges. A hundred sit ups. By the time he headed out into the cold, crisp air of the afternoon, he'd worked himself into a sweat.

The woman from the neighbouring cabin smiled at him as she carried her groceries in from the car. Hell, he needed supplies. He'd run for a couple of hours and get back before the supermarkets closed. The woman's brat screamed from the back of the car, his face red and furious, his little arms fighting the straps of the car seat. Raffaele snarled at him and hoped the little Bastard didn't make a habit of crying. A man had only so much patience.

The next day, Raffaele flicked up the shades of his glasses and settled himself at a table in the posh lobby of the Chateau. He ordered a coffee and opened the newspaper he found on the table, turning the pages with impatience. There was nothing about Lorenzo, and he smirked, scratching at the week-old scruff on his chin. He pulled the beanie off his head and stretched his toes inside his hiking boots.

His heart leapt and boogied when he caught sight of a tall fellow in black ski pants and a blue jacket, his face obscured. It had to be Dominico. He looked like a bouncer and his build was familiar—and his arm was slung around a leggy broad who had to be Abby Kercher.

He'd found them. Satisfaction bubbled in his veins like champagne.

Dominico appeared comfortable with his living arrangements. No prizes for guessing what went on behind closed doors. His brother always fell on his feet. It was one of the things Raffaele despised most about him. Along with the fact that Dominico had set up their mother like a queen in a fancy house, while Raffaele had rotted behind bars. Where was *his* weekly care package? No word, no sign of his Bastard brother for twenty long years. Nor of his God-damned father although he couldn't blame *him* for not wanting to visit. He doubted Dominico would recognise him. Twenty years in the slammer changed a man in obvious and not so obvious ways. Hatred was all that had kept Raffaele alive—that and his determination to make Dominico and Lorenzo pay.

Raffaele's coffee arrived and he took a sip, staring out of the window at the barren snow-covered landscape. It was a savage kind of scenery, and he could feel the power of it, like standing on the brink of creation. The earth wasn't quiet, it was raw and dangerous and prone to temper tantrums—a kindred spirit.

He took his time and read the paper from cover to cover, enjoying the piano music and the quiet that was to be had. When he was done, he drained his cup and sauntered out. He had a good sense of the layout of the hotel and he understood the movements of the staff. He'd done some research into the history of the building and he figured Dominico would have reserved the best room in the place, so that was a starting point for when he hacked into their system. He hadn't gotten to walk out of prison alive by skimping on the details.

A bus was waiting to take skiers and boarders up to the ski field and Raffaele slipped into the queue. He settled into a seat, and kept his scarf up around his face, his eyes hidden behind his lowered shades. His beanie covered his closely cropped hair. It would take a while to grow out. Prison meant a shaved head. No point having hair for some schmuck to grab a hold of.

Raffaele watched as Dominico and his whore-bitch got onto the bus. His brother's gaze skimmed over him and the skin on Raffaele's scalp tightened... nope. He was hidden in plain view. Just another tourist. Just another hotel guest.

He may as well travel up and scope out the ski area. And figure out what would work best.

Chapter Eight

Abby loved winter.

She loved the Alps in particular. On the chairlift with her neck warmer pulled up snug to her goggles, she could relax and soak in the magic of the mountain *and* the man beside her. Her fear of being found had settled over time… she had faith in Nico and his team. And out on the slopes their identities were well hidden by their ski-gear, which covered most of their faces.

They reached the top-station, and she hopped clear of the chairlift before plopping down to latch her boot back into the binding. She glanced at Nico who waited with a grin and pushed herself up, jumping her board into position on the side of the slope. The scenery stretched forever before them and the snow was pristine and squeaky. The sky was an endless blue and the sun shone, making every snow crystal sparkle.

"Are you ready?" Abby took a deep breath of the cold, fresh air, her stomach churning with nerves… or maybe it was excitement.

"Have been for aeons." Nico's words mocked her.

"I guess that's only fair since I'll have to wait for you at the bottom!" She tipped her board into the fall line and dived, carving huge arcs down the mountainside, her hand skimming the snow, the wind whistling in her ears. Defying gravity. Defying fear. She heard Nico behind her—and life didn't get better than this. She felt exhilarated and happy.

Here was spirit. Here was freedom. Here was conquest.

Two weeks into their retreat and she was surprised to find she'd pseudo-married the kind of man who paid attention to the small things. He was a gentleman in every sense of the word. As strong and reliable as the wall that divided their bed. He encouraged her without treating her like a child, challenged her without belittling her. He respected her independence. Not even the mountain misbehaved in his soothing, calming presence.

With no queues, they were back on the chair within minutes, and this time, when they arrived at the top, they planned to trek the hour-or-so climb up to the crater lake.

Fifty minutes into the hike and Abby wanted to dump her board onto the ground and strip off her winter woollies. But she refused to give Nico the pleasure of calling her a pampered princess... and she hated that his mocking voice was in her head.

She fixed her heated glare on the group of hikers in the distance ahead, like Lilliputians against the vast terrain and plodded on.

They made progress—slow progress—until finally, finally, they reached the top.

Here the mountain looked hotter than she was. Surrounded by meringue-like peaks of snow, the crater lake steamed like a witch's brew of silken turquoise. Incredible, unearthly beauty. If she could just catch her breath... she pulled her neck warmer away from her overheated body and stilled. It was quiet. The silence spoke of power, sacred and primitive, accentuated by the chilly blast of the wind, which was a welcome relief.

She dropped her board and tore off her gloves, goggles, and helmet. She fought for breath, her lungs grasping for oxygen, which was in short supply at this altitude. Her pulse was a rapid thud in her ears, and she dropped her hands to her knees, taking a moment to regroup.

"You're made of tougher stuff than I thought."

Hell no, she felt like a bedraggled kitten stuck up a too-high tree. "There's nothing tough happening here right now." She snatched at the frigid air for breath. "I think my heart's going to seize."

"I'm with you, princess. Let's hope one of us is up to administering mouth-to-mouth, or we're done for." He piled his stuff next to hers, his grin facetious.

"Don't call me that, and I thought mouth-to-mouth contact was off the agenda. Isn't that what the wall's about?"

"Mrs. Bortoli, you're far from good for a man's constitution."

"It was *your* suggestion to climb Mt. Everest here." His grin widened, and she couldn't help the hefty kick of reaction.

"I fully expected you to command me to carry your board. I thought you'd last about five minutes. You surprised me... in a good way."

"You don't think much of me if you thought I'd burden you with my board when you already had your skis."

"Not something a pampered princess would appreciate."

There it was again.

That back-handed maybe-compliment that cut her down at the same time as it patted her on the back. She got the message he didn't like who he thought she was—who she'd been—though why he found her father's money offensive when he had squillions of his own was beyond her.

"What is it, Nico? I can't help that my father's over-protective or that he's wealthy. Those are two things I have no control over. No more than you have any control over who *your* parents are."

She'd hit a raw nerve. She saw it immediately. He physically recoiled, his body stiffening and his fist curling.

What did she know about his past? Absolutely nothing. He was a blank canvas. He'd shared nothing of his own childhood, and he mocked hers at every opportunity. "Are your parents so much better than mine? Is that why you can't lower your standards to be with me?"

He choked. Physically choked until she thought he might require mouth-to-mouth. But then the jury was still out on whether he'd welcome her ministrations or prefer to expire. She suspected the latter. Damn the man to hell and back.

She turned away and focused her attention on the awe-inspiring scenery. Really, it was like being on top of the world.

Abby watched the small group ahead of them scale the highest part of the crater wall at a snail's pace. They'd been a moving target for her, but the gap between them had widened.

There'd be no such gap on the way back down. She'd been boarding with her father for as many years as she could remember. She was far from a speed fiend, but she was a good boarder, her skills honed from years of building technique and battling fear. She was as determined to master it on the slopes as everywhere else in her life.

And Nico could have helped her if he wasn't such a pig-headed man. The more time she spent with him, the more certain she was that she just needed to sleep with him to get over him. Master the fear. Ask him again. Beg him if she had to.

Hot tears defied the wind-chill and rolled down her cheeks. She fought the weakness, stiffened her spine, and stood strong against the wind that turned her heat to ice.

Lost in her own thoughts, she didn't immediately register the solid warmth of him when he came up behind her. Not until his arms closed around her, and he pulled her back against him.

"I want you more than I'm willing to admit, but we can't always have what we want. I appreciate that might be difficult for you to understand. Your father has always given you everything you want. And no, I'm not saying that's your fault."

The words were heated against the nape of her neck and there was tension in the hard muscle that pressed against her.

His warmth rippled through her like a sensual wave, seeping into her bones and leaving her weak. His musky scent pulled at her insides and left her jittery—shivery—vulnerable.

"He couldn't give me a mother who was brave enough to leave the house." Her words were quiet but sounded spoiled to her own ears. Maybe she was a pampered princess.

"At least she felt safe in her own home. That's more than my mother could say." His tone was bitter. "That's more than I could say."

His father had hurt him? And his mother? That explained Nico's drive to protect others. A wave of sympathy rose in her throat and she yearned to turn in his arms and hold him close, but instead she wrapped her arms more tightly around his and turned her cheek ever so slightly to brush against him. He'd never accept sympathy from her. She got that if nothing else. "Then you're nothing like your father."

Her gaze settled on the seething turquoise pool, and inside her body stirred and stormed. And then the words she'd missed—the words he'd distracted her from—found their way to the fore. He wanted her? *He wanted her.* She felt it in the fierce possession of his embrace.

"Perish the thought." Nico's body was taut.

"Tell me about him." She was afraid to move, afraid to spoil the fragility of the moment. She wanted to know more about him. She wanted to know what made him the way he was. Dangerous and safe. Ruthless and kind. Strong and tender. Detached. Remote. Courageous. So many words leapt into her head.

"This is far too beautiful a place to sully it with mention of my father. But my mother," his voice softened, "she would love it here."

"Your father sounds like a monster but look at the man you are despite him."

"But the man I am is rooted in my childhood, the same as the woman you are is rooted in yours. Isn't that why you work so hard to be independent?"

He'd aimed straight for the jugular. Abby broke out of his embrace and twisted around to face him. His eyes were an icy blue, but his gaze steamed like the crater lake behind her.

"You were the one who told me to make my life count for something."

His pupils flared despite the brightness, and the short space between them pulsed with an invisible force like a primordial drum. If she could have resisted him, she would have. She blamed the scenery—the isolation—the desolation that blasted through the Arctic wasteland of his eyes.

Her mouth found his—almost—and her lips swelled with the desperate need to close the miniscule gap. This was not a man to take what didn't belong to him. First, he would have to accept that she did belong to him. She challenged him to resist the frantic attraction that arced between them. Her heart clamoured against the wall of her chest—against the wall of his chest. Her pulse galloped, and when his surrender came, it was furious. Fierce. He dragged her against him and feasted with little ceremony.

She didn't want polite.

She wanted real.

She wanted him.

Nico devoured her. Demons inside him grappled with each other for more. He couldn't get enough of her. He couldn't stop the need to taste, to take, to savour, to sup.

This was no ordinary kiss. It punched into him like a comet exploding in the darkness of space. And like an addict welcoming back a long-resisted drug, he was lost in the magic of it. Her kiss promised hope and love and all things good... *his* made promises he couldn't keep.

Cravings deep and dark rattled the bars of their cage.

She met every ferocious stroke of his tongue with a passion as fiery and furious as his own. Their kiss was a duel, all flame and battle. A melding of souls. As primeval as the ground they warred on.

She wanted him. He wanted her. The solution was simple.

The solution was far from simple.

She'd fried his senses. What the hell was he thinking? He was her protector. Her guard. No person should be exploited by those meant to protect them. His conscience slammed into action and he pushed her away, inviting distance between them. He ran his thumb along the bruised softness of her lips and observed the bewilderment in her eyes.

"Abby, I…"

She didn't let him finish. "Don't you dare apologise. I won't let you." Her watery gaze held his, and he had the uncomfortable realisation that she could see right through him… to the pain he fought to hide. He'd deny it. He didn't need any woman's compassion. He didn't want it. He didn't deserve it. He couldn't risk it.

Nico lowered himself to the ground and grappled with the torn pieces of himself, pondering the hot liquid pool amidst the ice and snow. It should be damn well frozen over. The wind chill up here was cold enough to freeze living flesh.

Abby sat beside him, and they absorbed the beauty of the scenery in silence.

It was cold. It froze his fingers and seeped into his bones. He struggled to his feet and reached for Abby's hand.

"Come on, Abby. Let's get back." His face had turned to ice and cracked with the words.

He helped Abby to her feet—she looked as wretched as he felt—and rubbed her hands between his, the slight friction creating warmth, before he bundled them into her gloves. He settled her helmet onto her head and gazed into her defiant eyes. He couldn't stop the smile that started deep inside and bubbled to the surface.

With it came warmth.

She got under his skin and it irritated the hell out of him. Why she couldn't just do what was wise and stay clear of him he'd never know. "There's no need to pout."

"I'm not pouting." Her eyes were the same turquoise colour as the crater-pool and just as seething.

His smile turned into a chuckle. "You're pouting without a doubt."

"Pampered princesses pout."

"If the cap fits…"

"You're wrong about me." Her expression turned serious and he realised she was right. She was deeper and more complex than a lake that steamed hot when it should have been frozen.

He touched her chin. "You may be right."

He hefted his skis over his shoulder. It was a small trek to the crest and then downhill all the way to a warm shower and a glass of red wine.

He sure as hell had been wrong about how he thought she'd kiss. She kissed like a Jezebel, with no holds barred. The thought left him hard and uncomfortable. Damn the woman. She'd be the death of him one way or another.

Abby's heart ached.

Why wouldn't he give her what she wanted when it was what they *both* wanted? He'd kissed her back. He'd told her he wanted her.

So, maybe she was pouting.

Her board gave her wings and she swooped down the mountain towards the base of the ski area. She'd make him change his mind. But how?

His kiss had been intoxicating… addictive. To call it a kiss was to do it an injustice.

If they could generate that kind of heat with a kiss, what kind of heat would they ignite in bed? Enough to stop her freezing up? She had to know. She had to risk it. She had nothing to fear but fear itself.

The mountain had proved that fire could conquer ice, and if that could happen in nature?

Nico was a good man. To hell with the magazines and their

stories. She didn't care. She would trust her own judgement.

She may have gone about it unwisely five years ago, but she'd survived. And if this turned out to be a mistake, she'd survive this too. She was a survivor. She was tougher than she thought. The idea was a lovely one and it was Nico who had helped her to see it.

She wasn't weak. She had impressed him and now she wanted to woo him.

It would be a carefully orchestrated affair. She was a planner. Obsessive? Some might say that. Attentive was her own take on that part of her personality that liked to over-think things.

Maybe dinner downstairs? Yes, where she could discuss what she wanted without him jumping to his feet in a panic and rejecting her outright or retreating to his side of the Great Divide.

The grand dining room had a roaring fire and an elegant ambiance that spoke of intimacy. They were honeymooners and that was something she could use to her advantage. He could hardly act cold and distant when they were supposed to be in love.

Lovers would only have eyes for each other.

The more she pondered it the better she liked it. She'd seen the way his gaze followed her fork to her mouth and then deviated abruptly as if he'd been caught doing something wrong. Oh, yes, Nico D'Antoni. She may not be practiced in the art of seduction but that didn't rule her out of the game.

No. Tonight, the wall would fall. Perhaps the man had met his match after all. One thing was clear. One taste was far from enough.

One taste, and he was hooked.

Nico cursed the rapidly descending she-devil in front of him. Not only had she baited him, but she'd barbed her blessed kiss.

She'd got her message across loud and clear, and if she thought she had him on a platter, she had another think coming. He dug his edges into the snow, riding them fast and furious, the exhilaration of the descent marred only by the femme fatale outpacing him. She flew like a woman possessed.

Where was her caution? His lungs strained for oxygen and his muscles burned with lactic acid, yet still she plunged, her pace unfettered.

She was no angel; he could vouch for that! Nor was she the person he'd believed her to be. She was tough and resilient… more like her father than her mother. The thought gave him pause. He knew her father better than his own. If her father decided he wanted something, then nothing and no one could stand in his way. Fear ran cold in his veins.

How was he to resist her for another two weeks?

This went with the territory, his head argued. And witnesses were at their most vulnerable in the weeks leading up to the trial. The old teachings of his superiors were loud in his ears.

Now was the time to increase his vigilance, not relax it. Her very life depended on him staying focused. Her father depended on him thinking with his head and not with a less reliable part of his anatomy. Bob had entrusted him with the life of his daughter. It was a hefty responsibility.

To give in to the longings that coiled ever tighter inside him was unconscionable.

The fantasy had taken on a life of its own. Newly married couple celebrating their enduring love for each other.

Poppycock.

Marriage was a bitter and twisted place where love wilted

and died. He didn't need to make that mistake to know the territory. Love was fickle, and the women he dated knew it. The last thing he needed was to fuel the hopes of a princess living in fantasyland. In her world, princes rode to the rescue on snow-white stallions and slayed evil dragons. And starry-eyed couples lived happily ever after in rose-covered castles with love blooming all year round.

It had to stop. It had to stop, now.

Chapter Nine

B anging the snow from her boots, Abby pulled free of her gloves.

She'd hit the base of the Whakapapa ski area a good hundred metres ahead of he-who-could-not-be-beaten. It boded well for the rest of the evening.

"Nice of you to join me," she quipped as he showered her in a spray of snow, his skis slamming to a stop.

"Beaten by a daddy's girl." His tone told her exactly what he thought of that. If only he knew.

"You can leave my father out of it. He isn't here or haven't you noticed?"

"Oh, he's here alright."

"No, he isn't. It's just you and me." She snagged those blue, blue eyes and wouldn't let them go. "Stop using my father to push me away." Oh, he was going to find out how tough she was.

"What happened up there was unwise." His gaze didn't flinch. It was piercing and lethal and she didn't care how much he smouldered and sulked, if he thought he could scare her into changing her mind, he was wrong. "And dangerous. My job is to keep you safe."

Abby stepped out of her bindings and bent down to pick

up her board. She made her way onto the bus for the short ten-minute drive back to the Tongariro Chateau Hotel. He could say what he liked, but really, she didn't care anymore, because she'd learned to read his body language. He may have settled in silence beside her, but his body was as wound up as an over-tight spring and when he wanted something he couldn't have, a muscle ticked in his jaw like his conscience tapping its foot. She rattled him and the knowledge filled her with bravado.

He wanted her.

His wish was her command. He would have her—all of her. She would be cured of her teenage fantasies, and they could put this whole unwise attraction behind them.

His dark scowl deepened when they entered the drying room at the Chateau. "Abby, we need to stay vigilant."

She lowered herself onto a bench and eyed him like a praying mantis might eye its mate, her fingers fumbling with the straps on her boots.

"That won't happen again. You have my word."

Foolish man. "I'd rather your kiss." His kiss had intoxicated her. Devil-may-care had raced in her veins all the way to the base of the mountain... it raced in her veins still. She felt energised—super-powered.

"That was an error of judgement." He placed his skis in the rack and set to peeling off his jacket. It was over-hot in the small room compared with outside, and the air reeked from the damp boots on the boot heaters. Abby pulled off her helmet and stripped off her outer clothing for drying. She wriggled her feet out of her damp socks and reached for the hotel-branded slip-ons.

"Are you sure?" The question hung between them like a

sword ready to fall.

"Damn sure." His words were a growl.

"I'm not." Abby's tone was conversational. "Think about it, Nico. We're here for a two more weeks. It could be entertaining."

"You don't know what you're talking about."

"I know what I'm offering."

"You're in no position to offer anything. And I'm in no position to accept. You know why we're here."

The door opened and a couple came in on a blast of cold air, stomping the snow from their boots and cutting the conversation short.

"Did you have a good day?" The woman smiled with friendly warmth.

Abby smiled, her stomach twisting when she realised her face wasn't covered. It was her first interaction with anyone other than Nico in two long weeks. They were guests staying at the same hotel. There was nothing to fear. "The snow was amazing. How was your day?"

"Couldn't have been better." The woman grinned at her partner who banged the snow from his boots.

Abby lifted her neck warmer and half-covered her face and Nico tucked her in close to his side. "Have a lovely evening."

"We will. You, too."

Oh, we will, Abby vowed as they made their way out of the drying room and into the hallway. "I'm looking forward to a hot shower. How about you?" Nico tensed beside her, and she smiled to herself. Too easy. With her best poker face, she whispered. "Perhaps you'd like to join me."

Nico stopped and turned her towards him. "Be careful what you wish for. It just might come true."

Oh, that took the wind out of her sails. She twisted away and strode over to the lift doors. She pressed the up button more times than she needed to. Okay, so she had to tone it down, just a smidge. She was steering this ship and the last thing she needed was Nico at the controls. Then she'd be the one running scared. Her cocky bravado was rooted in his recalcitrance. His resistance fed her defiance, and her defiance fought her fear.

"I was joking." Her heart hammered in her ears. Surely, he wouldn't want to join her in the shower?

"It wasn't funny."

"I'm sorry. You're right. Getting naked with a man is a serious step." She blamed the adrenalin that raced through her veins and messed with her head for her sultry sarcasm.

He didn't answer until he'd closed the door to their room behind them and he had enough privacy to speak bluntly.

"Abby, getting naked with a woman I'm supposed to protect is negligence. Witnesses fall for those who protect them all the time. It's par for the course. This isn't your fault. It's what happens. It isn't real. It's fear looking for an escape route."

He sounded so sure of himself.

"Look at movies like *The Bodyguard*. Look at hostages who end up in love with the perpetrators of the crime against them. It's to be expected. I should have warned you."

Who was he trying to convince? "Perhaps you're right." Her battle plan could accommodate a backward step here or there. "This is about being forced to spend every waking and sleeping moment together."

"Exactly." He sounded relieved.

He shouldn't have. "Why don't we have dinner in the dining room tonight?" Her tone was breezy. "There's been no sign of danger and we don't want to raise suspicion by being too insular."

He considered her. "Maybe... okay. I think it's safe to do that. I'll head downstairs and organise it while you have your shower." His eyes mocked her, but she heard the word he hadn't voiced... alone, and she felt nothing but relief.

What had possessed her? She gathered her things and closed the bathroom door behind her. He'd awakened a part of her that had lain dormant for the past five years. The part that wanted him. And wanting him was a habit she needed to break.

She didn't want forever, did she? She stepped into the shower and twisted the faucet. The hot water pounded against her skin and she turned to savour the heat against her back. Forever was a long time. Forever was over-rated.

The threat of the pending trial and potential death had done one thing. It had underscored the many reasons why she shouldn't wait for him to come to his senses.

She might live and die waiting. She might live and die wanting. It had to stop, and there was only one way to put it to rest.

Nico didn't do forever. He would walk away. And she'd be free of her teenage fantasy. He'd implied their attraction was due to circumstance, and well fine, maybe he was right.

It wasn't like she wanted love. She knew he didn't believe in it. He chose his partners carefully to avoid it. But she was done with feeling second rate. For the past five years, she'd struggled to finish the deed with a single man... even with Gary, who she'd found attractive and lovely and caring. She needed to get Nico out of her system.

Lather oozed down her face, because... she'd used way too much shampoo. Turning her face to the water, she didn't hear him come in.

"Abby."

He wouldn't. He hadn't? Tell her, he hadn't opened the bathroom door. He'd see her silhouetted against the glass. Thank goodness for steam. Steam was a blessing.

"What is it?" Gulp. "Have you changed your mind?" What had possessed her? Why had she teased him? *Stop, Abby. Stop, right now.* Her heart flipped over in her chest.

"I'm going down to the bar for a drink." What was wrong with his voice?

He'd popped in to tell her he was leaving her alone? "Are you okay?"

"Yes… fine. I've booked dinner for seven. I'll be back in fifteen minutes or so."

"Okay, thanks." Her own voice sounded strained and she couldn't coordinate the muscles in her throat. She heard the door bang closed and she collapsed against the wall of the shower. Hell.

It was the first time he'd left her alone since they'd been here. So, neither one of them was ready to get naked. With the shampoo and conditioner rinsed, and the bathroom to herself, she turned off the faucet and reached for a towel.

Dry, but undressed, she revved up the hair drier and tousled her long hair into a mess of silky curls. She shadowed her eyes and darkened her lashes, accentuating the emerald green of her eyes. She observed her work with a critical eye and coloured her lips with rose-tinted gloss.

She brushed up okay.

With her towel wrapped tightly around her, just in case Nico came back, she padded across to the wardrobe and fossicked for the red dress she remembered seeing. The man had taste when it came to clothes and experience when it came to women.

She knew exactly who she was dealing with, and she knew how to dress the part. She'd observed. She'd learned. Men like Nico were deliciously wild. They moved from woman to woman like lust-driven nomads. Maybe lust was enough.

Heaven knows she'd lusted after him for years. At twenty, she'd stupidly told him she loved him. No wonder he'd thought her a naïve and spoiled little rich girl. What had she been thinking?

Baby steps she reminded herself. She would deal with the lust. And leave love for another day.

The lounge area was busy with groups of people relaxing to the sound of the baby grand piano. Nico's nerves leapt as a rack of balls scattered on the full-sized billiard table. It wasn't like him. He fully blamed Abby and that kiss. Not to mention the shared shower proposition. Two weeks in close company with Abby Kercher had him on the verge of madness. Wanting what he couldn't have was clouding his judgement and his danger radar was off. Hell, his whole system was under siege.

He greeted the barman and lowered himself onto a stool at the bar. "Scotch on the rocks, thanks, mate." The young fellow had the demeanour of someone on a working holiday. His hair was dyed blonde and spiked in every direction. Nico scanned the room and found nothing out of the ordinary, but then they'd hardly spell it out for him.

"Did you head up to the mountain today?" The fellow placed Nico's drink down in front of him.

"Yeah, thanks, we did. The skiing was awesome, and we hiked up to Crater Lake, which was out of this world."

"Yeah, it's totally sick up there."

"Is that an Aussie accent?"

"Yep, I'm over here for the season." He grinned. A couple seated themselves a short distance away and he excused himself to serve them. Nico listened to their brief conversation and sipped his drink. He didn't plan on finishing it. He needed his wits about him with Abby on planet romance.

Taking his drink with him, he wandered towards the foyer to use the lobby phone. He jabbed in the numbers for his next in charge. "Jarrod. Talk to me. What's new at your end?"

"Hi, Boss. Glad you called in. Your brother's parole application was fast-tracked, and he got out nearly two weeks earlier than we anticipated... he's gone to ground. I've got Doug working on locating him, but until we find him, you'll need to be doubly vigilant. Abby's group have been busy, too."

"Another heist?"

"Yeah. They got ten kids out. It was in the Thai news. Word is the big players are mighty pissed-off. Is everything okay there? Do you need more men on the ground?"

"I don't want to risk anyone finding us. So far, there's been no sign of trouble. I'll let you know if that changes."

Nico lowered the receiver and took a slow sip of his drink. *Raffaele was out.* The three words hit him like a grenade to the chest. He hadn't seen his brother in two decades... and it was only a matter of time until his brother came looking for him.

Nico didn't like it. He didn't like it at all.

He scanned the lounge area. The guests who had gathered for an après ski drink looked relaxed and jovial. There was no sign of his brother and the twist in his abdomen began to ease. Maybe Abby was right. Maybe getting away from the close confines of their room would ease the tension that clouded his judgement.

Besides, he could usually smell danger from a hundred metres down the road. If danger came close, he'd know about it.

Nico lowered his near empty glass to the bar and headed for the lift. His mind shifted to Abby in the shower... naked and streaming with water. The torturous image was etched into his memory bank and no matter how hard he tried to erase it, it pulled at him like a magnet. What demon had possessed him? He'd fought to keep his eyes on neutral space, but they'd fought back, determined to feast themselves silly. As if they didn't have enough problems.

Nico stepped out of the bathroom and observed Abby's quiet figure in the window seat. Her attention was glued to the dark scenery beyond. He'd changed into casual pants and a cashmere top. "Are you ready for dinner?"

"Yes, I'm looking forward to it. I think I've got cabin fever."

"Me, too, to be honest, but it's a once-off so let's make the most of it."

He held the door open for her and was accosted by her fresh womanly scent, all spice and nice. Her figure was dynamite in the red dress he'd selected for her and her hair rippled with vitality, all shine and silky softness. She smiled and held his gaze, and he near jammed his fingers in the door. Damn the little minx. She couldn't be oblivious to the effect she had on him. It would be good to get out of their room, which had become a too small, too cosy, too intimate hell-for-his-senses.

He wrapped his arm around her and felt the rigidity in her spine. Was she worried it wasn't safe? "I've checked who's down there and whilst it's a calculated risk, I think we should be okay." She smiled up at him and a wave of warmth washed through him.

"I feel safe here despite my initial concerns." She wrapped her arm around him and snuggled close sending his own body into spasm. They stepped into the lift and he pushed the button for the lobby.

"You must be hungry. We worked hard today." His heart hammered like he'd just skied a black run and pulled up a full hundred metres behind Abby despite pushing himself to the limit.

"We did."

Physical exhaustion was Nico's main defence. He skied like a madman on the mountain each day and fell into an exhausted sleep each night, his body too tired to battle Abby's she-devil presence on the other side of the bed.

If he'd chosen an island resort, they'd have had a major problem. He'd have breached the damn wall in less than five minutes.

He pulled her close and breathed in the fresh and sweet scent of her hair. The lift doors opened, and they walked towards the dining room. Nico's heart thudded while he scoped the space, but all appeared okay and he breathed easier.

"Mr. and Mrs. Bortoli, how lovely to see you. Did you enjoy your day on the slopes?"

"Very much, thank you." Abby was quick to chime in, while Nico was still sifting through the sights and sounds.

"We hiked up to the crater lake. It was so beautiful and desolate up there."

"You must have worked up an appetite."

"Indeed, we did," Nico selected a table for two by the window, not far from the warmth of the beautiful old fireplace, but away from the centre of the room.

"I'll bring some warm bread while you look at the menu."

"We'd appreciate that." Nico sat with his back to the window so he could see the room, his skin alert for any prickle of unease. Abby's gaze was on the menu.

A tea light burned in a small crystal bowl on the table between them, casting a romantic glow across the vintage lace tablecloth and crystal glassware. Fine dining. Good wine. It was the perfect place for a honeymoon. Perhaps the only one he'd ever experience.

Abby wouldn't be so keen to breach the wall if she knew about Raffaele and his role in her mother's post-traumatic stress disorder. Raffaele chose a life of crime before he'd even left school—first in juvenile justice and then prison. Where evil had a way of spreading.

Nor would she be so interested if she'd seen his mother's bloodied face and bruises after copping a hiding at the hands of his devil-spawn father. No woman deserved to be bullied by a man and no bully deserved the love of a woman.

"This is lovely." Abby glanced up, her movements relaxed and casual.

She appeared oblivious to the pull of sexual attraction that had him hard and wanting. Wanting what he couldn't have.

"What do you feel like tonight?" Her gaze pierced him like an arrow and the husky edge in her voice raised his discomfort level another notch. He deserved eternal damnation for the direction of his thoughts. She was like a ripe, shiny apple sent straight from the Garden of Eden to tempt him.

Eyes down. Eyes on the menu. Eyes off the gorgeous woman.

"I'd like to try the spatchcock." Was it his fraught imagination or had she really emphasised that word the way he feared she had?

Nico struggled to focus on the menu in front of him. "It does look good." His voice wavered. Damn the woman. She was playing with him. "But it was a tough day, so maybe the Steak au Poivre for me." He needed strength and iron in his blood.

"Yes, it was." Her gaze held his over the menu. "I'm looking forward to bed tonight."

Her eyes danced with a thousand sparkling lights... but she didn't look tired. She looked like a woman with seduction on her mind, which was ridiculous. He was losing his touch. There was an art to reading a woman, and he was usually a master. If his instincts were on the money, he was in for a big night.

Over his dead body.

The waitress lowered a basket of warm crusty bread rolls into the middle of the table, along with a pad of butter and a small saucer of olive oil.

"Are you ready to order? Would you like champagne first?"

"Oh, yes, please. I'd love a champagne." Abby's green eyes flashed, and her voice curled around his heart like a fist.

"What about you, sweetheart?"

Sweetheart? If she only knew what horrors lurked in that part of his anatomy. "That sounds perfect, thank you." He'd rather a beer, but tonight was about Abby.

The waitress took down their orders and smiled. "I'll be right back with the champagne."

Abby shifted her gaze to his. "Our honeymoon has been fabulous so far, and I couldn't appreciate it more." She reached over and took his hand, circling her thumb around his palm.

His body jerked, but he could hardly pull his hand away. They were newlyweds. And it was then that he saw his mistake.

Her hand swept along his forearm, her touch intimate and warm. His senses rioted and it was then that he knew he was toast.

Her fingers curled around his—soft, but firm. "We both know where this is headed."

"I've been more than clear about where this is headed, and where it isn't." He pulled his hand away in the guise of removing his jacket, and she had no choice but to remove hers. She smiled a secret smile, and he cursed the heat in the room. It was hot. He reached for the jug of chilled water and poured some into Abby's glass before filling his own.

He lifted the glass to his mouth and gulped, the delicious chill quenching the parched terrain of his throat.

Abby spread butter onto a piece of bread roll and sank her teeth into it. His body reacted as if she'd sunk her teeth into his flesh.

The waitress returned with their champagne, giving him a brief reprieve before the torture of the evening continued.

"Abby." He couldn't very well tell her to back off. Not here in the public domain of the restaurant. Mr. and Mrs. Bortoli were on their honeymoon. She had him. She'd outwitted him, and the slight jut of her chin told him loud and clear that she knew it.

"Yes, my love."

Love? He loaded his eyes with behave-you-minx-or-else. Hers widened with feigned innocence.

"Here's to the rest of our honeymoon." He raised his glass and waited for her to lift hers. "May it be uneventful."

"And to everlasting love." Her smile was smug.

"And to an early night." He smiled back, digging deep.

"And to the fall of the wall." Dimples appeared in the soft

pink of her cheeks and his heart banged a warning.

"That's not going to happen." Damn the woman to hell and back. She would regret this. He would regret this.

The evening charged away, given free rein by a beautiful princess who didn't have the first clue about what was good for her.

When the entrée arrived, his certainty began to slip. Would it really affect her safety if he was to give her what she begged for? She'd be safer in his arms than out of them. His mind was a slippery eel, throwing valid rationalisations for every desire that rose with the lift of her dark lashes, the swipe of her rosy tongue across her shiny pink lips—moist, plump, and inviting.

By the time dessert appeared, his resolve was a weakened old man, rickety and precarious. Her spoon was an implement of torture with every sexy slide of it over her lips—lips as luscious as forbidden fruit. His gaze followed the sweep of her tongue, transfixed by the sweet wickedness of her mouth. And she knew it. She played up to it. She exaggerated it. She'd challenge the resolve of a saint.

"Coffee?" His voice cracked.

"Yes." She responded too quickly. Where was the sultry Jezebel? Why did her eyes seek refuge in the distance over his shoulder?

"I thought you were in a hurry to get to bed." What devilry had seized his faculty of thought?

"I thought you wanted to delay it as long as possible." Her teeth pressed into her lip and then he realised. She was afraid. The valiant knight within him charged to victory.

"You've changed your mind."

"No, I haven't." Her words were a lie. "Have you?"

All he had to do was say yes, he'd changed his mind. "No."

Relief sprang into her eyes. She was vulnerable. She was in his care. He wouldn't take advantage of that. Not if it killed him.

"That game you play is a dangerous one." That game she played was deadly. A battle ground. Tonight, he'd won, but she was dynamite. He needed sleep.

"Let's go home." Home. It was a word that settled around him like a comforter.

"Yes." Her answer was simple, but it harboured more meanings than he cared to ponder.

Darkness.

With the light out, thoughts pummelled him from every quarter. Sleep was a distant thing, sullen and uncooperative, and the silence howled like a ghost.

The wall was solid and high. He visualised its strength creating a thicket of thorns in his mind... an impenetrable barrier, impossible to scale.

But then he caught a sound. Stifled. His ears raked the silence until he was sure he'd imagined it. There. There it was again. Abby was crying? He held his breath, the need to breach the wall was suddenly urgent and difficult to resist.

"Abby, are you awake?"

"No."

He grinned despite the battle brewing within him. The woman was a torment. "Do you want to talk about it?"

Was he insane? He didn't do bed-talk. Bed-talk was a minefield he'd learned to navigate with the utmost of care. It required wily manoeuvres he wasn't up to tonight. He was battle-worn. Weary. Not on his game.

"No, but thanks." The last word caught on a sharp intake

of breath. A sob. She was in pain? It was like someone had driven a blade into his own flesh.

"What is it? Are you worried about the trial? We're safe here. You're safe with me."

The sobs started afresh, more obvious now, more wrenching.

"Abby, it's okay."

"No, no, it's not."

"It will be. I promise. You'll give your evidence, and those blackguards will be imprisoned. You've been incredibly brave. What you did for those children—what you do for Project Karma is amazing.'

He was surprised to find he meant it. Really meant it. He admired her. He respected her. She'd become a woman of integrity. A woman of steel. A woman of fire. The kind of woman who could reach inside a man and touch his soul. "Abby, talk to me." Damn the wall. Her sobs drove him to the brink of surrender.

"Nico…" The word was barely audible over the noise that roared in his ears.

"I need your help."

"You know I'm here for you." Anything. He'd do anything if she'd just stop crying. This was the last frontier. It would be so easy to knock the blasted cushions from here to Hades, but the wall was all that kept them safe from each other.

"I'll make you a hot chocolate." He grappled in the dark for the switch on the bedside lamp.

"No." Her tone was urgent.

"You don't want a hot chocolate?"

"No, I don't want the light on."

Chapter Ten

This was hard enough in the dark. There was no way Abby could tell Nico what she needed to tell him under the glare of light. She was exposed enough.

She had to take the risk and let him decide whether he was willing to help her. But how could she look him in the face and maintain her self-respect if he refused her? What if he didn't? What then? What if there really was something wrong with her?

He'd offered to make her a hot chocolate?

Her heart melted and her sobs deepened. He was kind and thoughtful and caring. The kind of man who built a wall to protect a woman's virtue. The kind of man who stayed on the other side of the wall because that was the right thing to do.

How could she ask him to go against what he believed was right?

What kind of playboy bachelor shared a bed with a woman—a willing woman—and stayed on his own side?

She'd offered herself to him on a platter. Was she so distasteful? Was she so unattractive to him?

No. He was attracted to her. He wanted her.

"What sort of help?" Nico spoke quietly, his tone soothing and intimate.

She added patient and gentle to the list. "I need you to hear me out... before you say, no." Tears coursed down her cheeks and her heart leapt in her breast. There was no movement from the other side of the bed. No sound. Had he balked at the first hurdle?

Damn the man, this wasn't working. She sat up and pulled at the wall between them. Yanked at the cushions, her tears spilling without check, her sobs louder now, more insistent.

"Abby, that is a really bad idea." His voice was tight with restraint.

"Nico, I need you to hold me. I'm sorry, I know..." The words were lost in the emotions that tore at her throat. "I know you don't want me..." Sobs. A volley of them racked her body until she shook like a leaf. And then the cushions were gone, and Nico was there, his shoulders rounded and hard, his chest bare and curved, his face wary.

"Abby, that's not true." He drew her into his arms and held her tight against him, his body hot and hard.

"I do want you. That's the problem." He murmured the words into her hair and his lips pressed against her forehead. She nestled in against him and allowed his strength and his heat to seep into her.

Hard muscle. A beast of a man. A gentle beast of a man. She ran her lips over his jaw—square and rough—and turned her cheek to brush against his. Her breath flew, fast and furious, and her heart hammered.

Nico's breath was jagged, and he lay rigid, his body near vibrating.

"Nico, I need..." She bit her lip with frustration. How the hell did she put this into words?

He pulled away and brushed the tears from her cheeks,

before lowering his mouth to within a breath of hers. His eyes were dark and stormy and intensely focused.

She squeezed her own eyes closed. She didn't want him to see what she knew he would see there... her desire for him, raw and aching.

In the end it was *she* who closed the miniscule distance, *he* who tasted with a soft caress as if he cared, *she* who tasted back, supping delicately of his strength as heat brewed and curled in the centre of her body. With flames of need growing and blasting every thought of caution, they feasted on each other—feasted and gorged.

She wanted. She needed. She'd leave love for another day.

There was only a thin layer of nightwear between them. Her hands scooted over his body, over lean muscle, stopping here and there to trace the irregular feel of a scar. Over curves and valleys, planes, and edges. A tantalising landscape that her hands devoured.

He made no move to rush.

He let her direct the pace.

He met every slide of her hand over his body with a guttural groan as if her slightest touch was the worst kind of agony—the best kind of bliss. She lowered her mouth to his scars and kissed the flaws. What terrible pain had he suffered at the hands of his father? Her heart tore and she yearned to salve the long-ago hurt. He buried his hands in her hair with a moan, and she heard her own answering sob as his hands travelled over her skin.

He pulled her closer and held her tight... and her tears started afresh. He'd been hurt, his body traumatised. She'd never communed with a man like this. Her tears were for him. He stroked and soothed and eased, and his gentle touch allowed the tension inside her to slowly unfurl. She lost herself in the promise of his kiss.

Here was safety.

Here was a man who would understand if she gave him the chance.

She clamoured closer and he chuckled, a deep vibration she felt against her chest. She wanted all of her body to touch all of his. Their legs tangled together, and he dragged her against him as if the smallest gap was an unbearable separation.

He settled his mouth on hers, possessive and greedy, and deepened his kiss. Longing rippled through her and gathered like a storm, a thundering ache inside her. She ground her body against his, instinctively in time with the provocative stroke of his tongue… and the rhythm of their kiss ramped up.

Abby wanted to rush but Nico lingered. She was on fire from the inside out. She sensed his body was as wound up as hers—but his touch was as languid as a summer breeze.

He lifted her pyjama top, his hand sliding against her feverish skin, and she rushed to get it over her head, and gone. She wriggled out of her pyjama bottoms in half a moment and pressed against him. She wanted to feel him. All of him. Skin-to-skin. Desire had spots dancing before her eyes, her blood barrelling around, too fast, too loud.

Never had she been so hell-bent on relieving a man of his pants. She pushed at the fabric and he chuckled anew.

"What's the rush?"

"I want you. Now. Before you change your mind." Want wasn't a strong enough term.

"I want you too, but you know this is an exceptionally bad idea, right?"

"It's an exceptionally good idea." Her hand skimmed over

the curve of his chest, the moonlight revealing his tattoo. It was the only ink on his tanned torso. "What does the bird represent?"

"Escape from the darkness." His voice thrummed against the nape of her neck and lifted the follicles on her skin. He reached for the light.

"Don't put the light on." Her words arrowed into the air between them. She didn't want him to destroy the comfort of the shadows. She had hang ups and lots of them and she'd rather not feel spotlighted when she built the courage to tell him.

"Trust me, I can see you. The moonlight's bright." His hand rested on the small of her back, venturing lower over the curve of her buttock.

"The moonlight I can live with."

"You don't want me to see you naked?"

"It's not that. I like the darkness. With you. I like the *feel* of you."

"Oh, I like the feel of you, too." He pulled her closer and pressed hot and pistol hard against her. "And trust me, it's not like I haven't seen you naked before—in my mind's eye."

"You have?" She pulled away to study his face—the shadows and the light—resting her palm against his cheek, the dark stubble soft against her hand.

"Of course. I'm a man and you're a particularly attractive woman."

She gathered the shreds of her confidence around her. He was the only man she'd ever truly desired and to know that he wanted her, too, was the most wonderful of gifts.

Nico drew her back into the cradle of his arms, and she savoured his musky male scent. He was hot, deliciously hot, and when he pulled her close, her breasts crushed against the rough hair of his chest, the delightful friction making them swell and harden.

She was sodden with her need for him, but he meandered when she wanted to race. His mouth left hers to trail along the line of her neck creating an electric current that arced through her body. His hands cupped her breasts, hot and wicked, and the sensual storm inside her grew from rumbling to booming, his touch lighting spot fires all over her body.

Her back arched up off the mattress when his mouth moved to her breasts, the fiery lick of his tongue sending arrows of sensation to that intimate part of her that throbbed with impatience.

Every possessive taste took her closer to the edge, his hands charged with a magical force. And when he finally cupped his hand over her mound, his fingers easing into her slick folds, she roared up and over the precipice of an orgasm like none she'd experienced before. She soared with Nico's breath against her skin, his groan in her ears.

She collapsed back and gasped for air, completely drained as aftershocks racked her body. Her chest heaved like she'd just hurtled down Mt. Ruapehu in record time.

Wow. Her head spun with the wonder of it.

Nico drew her close and dragged the covers up and over them. They lay together and the thump of her heart gradually steadied, until it occurred to her that he planned to settle into sleep. He'd given her pleasure like none she'd ever known—given her comfort like none she'd ever known—and had no expectation of reciprocal rights. What kind of pampered princess did he think she was? Did he think she'd snuggle into him and say, thanks a bunch? Sleep well. His opinion of her sucked. "Nico."

"Hmmmm?"

"Are you planning to go to sleep?"

"You must be tired."

"And you must be crazy if you think I'm not going to finish what I started."

"There's no need. You needed comfort, and we don't need this to get any more complicated than it already is." His voice vibrated from deep within his chest. She felt him hard and heavy against her hip.

"I know you think the timing's all wrong and that I'm an over-indulged princess, but I'm begging you. I need to get you out of my head. I need to know that I can be with a man without... freezing up. Nico, please..." Her voice trailed off as she lost her courage. As tears started to spill. Please, please don't roll away. "I need to do this."

Silence.

She'd told him—she'd begged for his help—and he had nothing to say? She'd embarrassed him. She'd embarrassed herself. She'd made him feel awkward—no more awkward than she felt right now. If he didn't say something soon, she would implode with humiliation. But he had to know, she had to tell him, before he found out by default, or he would blame himself and it would be even more difficult to face him in the morning. She'd started this showdown, and she had to finish it.

"Nico, please." Fear tore the words from her throat. Please don't say no. Please don't reject me. Please don't freeze me out.

Please body, don't freeze *him* out.

Oh, God, it was a mess. A mess she couldn't see her way

out of. He'd probably decide it was all too hard. She was high maintenance. Hard work. An uphill battle, not a downhill race to the finish line.

He liked his women, practiced and promiscuous. Not pathetic. What had she been thinking? Why would he want her... especially now?

Tears coursed down her face and she swallowed against the sob that swelled in her throat. Why did she have to spoil the moment? It had been going so well. Why had she said anything? She might have been able to bluff her way through it. He may never have known? He'd given her an orgasm like none she'd ever experienced before. It might have been fine and now her body would freeze up as surely as if she had frigid tattooed across her forehead.

Hell.

She didn't dare speak in case she said the wrong thing.

She didn't dare move in case he pushed her away and rebuilt the wall. She wanted to stay in the heaven of his arms. He'd think she was as mad as her mother.

Damn it. She wouldn't let fear control her. She needed to do this. With Nico. She had to. This was no longer an option. This was mandatory. Urgent. Necessary.

He couldn't say no.

What had she just said?

Nico trawled through the desire-saturated recesses of his brain trying to grapple with the meaning of her words, words he could never have anticipated in his wildest dreams.

She *froze up* with men? Physically?

All he was conscious of was the immeasurable bliss of Abby in his arms. Her body fitted against his like it was made to be

116

there. The curve of her back against his chest, her buttocks tight and perky nestled into the crook of his body. Her screams still echoed in his mind—her orgasm had filled his senses and hardened his groin to the point of explosion. If she so much as wriggled her hips, he would humiliate himself like a schoolboy.

He needed a moment to compose himself. To regain control of his body, which was charged and ready to fire.

She curled away from him. Crying? "Abby. It's alright." What was going on? His brain just couldn't catch up. He needed to focus. This was important.

"I'm sorry." Abby's voice broke.

"Don't be sorry." Was she insane? She'd just driven him to heights of pleasure he'd never known. The women he usually bedded were intent on seducing and impressing. Rare indeed for a woman to lose herself in his touch until he felt like a genie, so powerfully magic he could move the earth and the heavens.

He scooped her closer and nuzzled his mouth into the curve of her neck. She tasted like nectar. Her hair was honey sweet and her skin was musky with a scent that was Abby's alone. It had his senses soaring into the stratosphere, his blood coursing south. Not good. He needed to think.

Thinking wasn't possible. Not with Abby naked against him, her skin satiny smooth, her hair silken and soft, her body as snowy white as porcelain.

She shook with emotion and his mouth sought hers, to reassure, to savour, to soothe.

Whatever it was, he would make it right.

The desire to protect her was fierce. He wanted to claim her for his own. To prove to her that she was the most beautiful woman on the planet.

But to sleep with Abby was not a flash-in-the-pan proposition. She would demand so much more. More than he'd ever given before. More than he had to give?

He couldn't fight her. To hear her pain—to know her pain—*to know the source of her pain*—and do nothing was not an option.

Her lips clung to his. This was a branding, intense and raw. She grappled with his emotions as surely as her tongue twisted with his, and her sobs wrenched his insides. He loaded his kiss with all the things he couldn't say. Not if he wanted to keep her safe. Not if he wanted what was best for her.

At some level, he accepted the inevitable. Abby was a force as unwavering as the earth beneath them.

Her hand travelled an erotic path over his back, searing him like flame or melted wax, and the need to lose himself in her heat was a roar in his ears but this wasn't about him. He steeled his resolve—gasped aloud when her hand closed around him, tentative and tantalising.

She ran her fingers along his length and circled the tip with the pad of her finger, skimming over nerve endings that stormed with desire.

"Nico, I want you, but I…"

"You're perfect." He hushed her, his words a vibration across her lips, swollen with his kisses. Her scent drove him to distraction, his head filling with Abby and his need to give her pleasure.

She wriggled against him, manoeuvring him closer to the pulsing wetness between her thighs. He fought the fire in his body… pressed gently against her—slowly—slowly separating her folds, waiting, waiting. He lowered his hand to touch the tightened nub that pressed against him… slow and easy. Sighs.

Soft sighs as she thrust her hips into his touch, her ascent steady and sure.

Impatience screamed in every cell of his body, but he was lost in the pleasure of hers. Every sigh, every breath, every groan. He wanted her to scream his name. He wanted her to break around him in an orgasm like none she'd ever experienced before. He wanted her to remember this moment forever in the best possible way. He wanted her to feel complete and whole and healed.

Her body flowered and swelled around the pulsing head of his erection... liquid heat, fiery resistance. He rolled her onto him and gave her the reins, encouraging her to ride him, to take her time.

There was fear in the short gusts of her breath, and he lifted his mouth to hers, taking his time to reassure and coax. With one hand on the perfect curve of her bottom, and the other tangled in the silken magic of her hair, he deepened his kiss and gave all that he had.

Abby pressed back, moved away, pressed back again, sending him into crazy land. He held on, tempering the need to rush, allowing the agonising friction to build and build until he thought he might shatter from wanting her...

And then his head shifted a gear and it struck him.

He hadn't used protection. "Abby... I need to get... condom." Where the hell was his wallet?

"On the pill..." Her words were a pant, her mouth seeking his, stealing his words and the sense from his head.

Her pace quickened and she cried out, the silken barrier inside her breaking away. With his entry no longer hindered, he sank deeper, too late to pull back, too late to do anything but hold on. Desire coiled inside him, demanding, stampeding, and caution was a distant yell from the sidelines.

Every sensual glide of her body against him, every thrust, every speeded up shift of her weight took him closer to the brink, and when her velvet sheath clamped around him and she screamed his name, the volley of contractions like machine gun fire, he could no more stop the orgasm that blasted through him than resist Abby's pleas, so powerful and irresistible was its force. Higher than he'd ever been thrown, so far into the stratosphere that his spirit soared with hers.

Pure bliss. Pure sensation. Pure heaven.

His heart stopped for an eternity. And when it thundered back into life, kick-starting his brain and dragging him back from the heavens, he held her close. Close to his heart. Close to the small boy inside him who yearned for love but feared he didn't deserve it.

What had they done?

He was the worst kind of fraud.

They'd had unprotected sex. Even if she was on the pill. He hadn't kept her safe. *Her* first time. *His* first time *without a condom.*

"Abby…" He forced the blackness away, clung to how right she felt in his arms. "Are you okay?" Had he hurt her? He couldn't bear the thought and rained kisses on her head. Was she okay? "Abby?"

She stirred in his arms where she lay heavy and limp, as shattered as he felt. She lifted her head and settled her lips against his. "Oh, yes. Thanks to you."

The words were a whisper, a vibration against his hypersensitive skin. Her sigh mingled with her tears and she breathed him in, her kiss numbing his mind to anything but her taste.

Eyes closed, arms around her, his body melded with hers,

he thought he'd died and gone to heaven. Later, he'd worry about his responsibilities. Right now, he just wanted to be. In the moment. With Abby.

It didn't get better than this.

This was her Everest. He was her man. She knew it with every fibre of her being. She'd gifted him her soul.

Not only had their bodies joined—joined—he'd possessed her like he'd been made for her and her alone.

Atoms had shifted. Molecules had parted.

She drank him in greedily. Fully addicted. She couldn't get enough. She wanted more. She wanted to gorge herself silly.

He filled her. He completed her. She savoured the feel of him inside her. Fully inside her. She wanted him to stay there forever. She wanted the moment to last forever.

He rolled them onto their sides. "I could stay inside you forever," he whispered, his voice ragged.

The words warmed her like sun-heated river stones against her skin. "I wish you could." Her emotions roller-coasted between sublime happiness and grief and everywhere in between. Tears threatened again and she bemoaned her weakness.

With Nico, she'd conquered her fear. She should be ecstatic. She should be freed. Instead, she was weak. Weak with wanting a man she couldn't truly have. Weak because suddenly his body was not enough. She wanted his heart. She wanted every dark, secret corner of him. She ached with her need for him.

Stupid, foolish, naïve girl.

Get over it. He'd given her what she'd begged for and she had no right to demand more. If he could do this for her against his better judgement, the least she could do was accept his terms. He'd already given her more, so much more than she had a right to ask for. So much more than she could ever repay.

"Abby, this complicates things."

Complicated was the understatement of the century. She had to let him off the hook. This had been her idea. He'd resisted her until she'd left him no option. No man was immune to a naked woman. That much she'd learned.

"This doesn't need to be complicated." She could be mature about this. They were attracted to each other. A brief affair was what she would offer. No strings. Walk away at the end of the trip. What happens on the mountain, stays on the mountain. His terms.

"Abby…"

"Mr. and Mrs. Bortoli should be allowed to have marital sex. It goes with the territory. No reason why Abby and Nico should get in the way of that."

"Are you proposing what I think you are?" His voice fractured.

"Why not? I think you enjoyed it as much as I did. Didn't you?" Fear gripped her by the throat. Oh, my God. What if he hadn't? What if she'd been so lost in her own pleasure, she hadn't paid attention to his? What if he'd just humoured her? What if she'd come across as a beginner? The what if's circled her head like crows.

"Are you crazy?" He drew her closer, his body swelling inside her until their fit was seamless. He rocked her pelvis against him, and fires flared where embers had burned. Oh, he knew how to drive a woman to distraction.

"I am now." Her words were short and snatched from the air.

"You want to have a physical relationship for the duration of our trip?"

"I do." The vow was as ancient as time… albeit a short time for them.

"I usually wear a condom for health reasons as well as contraceptive ones…"

Oh, hell, she hadn't thought of STDs. Her mind had been so filled with her fear of the physical act, her ecstasy, her triumph; she hadn't given a thought to the practicalities. And she hadn't given him a chance. It had been so spontaneous. So ravenous. So emotional.

"I haven't been with anyone else." And then it struck her. He wasn't the one at risk. She *was* immature and inexperienced. But she didn't plan to spell that out for him in capital letters. He was a confirmed bachelor, and she'd do well to remember it!

He didn't play for keeps.

"And I've always worn a condom—always—so in that case…" He traced his hands over her breasts, the tension building again, and rolled her onto his chest. She couldn't resist the urge to rock her hips, to move against him, to stoke the fire that burned like flame.

He took her face in his hands and she fell into the blue depths of his eyes. He drew her mouth back to his and she smiled against his lips. "In that case, I can have my wicked way with you. Again." Abby nibbled at his lip and ran her chin along the scratchy terrain of his. She nestled her nose alongside his, her skin craving the touch of his.

And when his strong, masculine hands grazed the length of her spine and cupped the flesh of her buttocks, her breasts crushed against the soft wiry hair on his chest. Her entire body was alive to his. Alive to his touch. Alive to the sensations that wreaked havoc from the inside out and the outside in.

Her heartbeat hammered against the wall of her chest. She devoured his mouth, her tasting possessive, her hunger fuelling his. He rolled her onto her back and took control of the pace, and Abby basked in the thrill of his body, muscular and powerful. He moved slowly—rhythmically—until her groans became cries, until she rocked her hips faster and harder, until he reached down, and his provocative touch sent her flying into orbit, her scream ringing in her ears, her heart pounding with emotion.

And when he pinioned her hips and his orgasm fired inside her, the aftershocks sent a barrage of stars into a sky already filled with fireworks. He collapsed against her, his groan of bliss melding with hers.

Oh, could it get any better? This was what she'd craved. This connection. This incredible intimacy.

Her heartbeat banged and her blood rushed in her ears as she slumped back into the pillow.

"My God, Abby."

Nico rolled them onto their sides and snuggled her close. The aftermath was as earth shifting as the main event. She felt cosseted and safe and precious and special. Call her crazy. She was crazy. Crazy with wanting him. Crazy with loving a man who didn't do love.

Chapter Eleven

Nico cussed and cursed and called himself every kind of cad. In the light of day, he could see himself for the scoundrel he was. What had seemed irrefutably right in the shadows of the night, with Abby's sobs loud in his ears, now seemed predatory. What kind of man took advantage of a woman he was supposed to protect? Maybe it had all been an elaborate hoax? She'd been so far from freezing as to be ridiculous. Maybe she'd been smart enough to know to appeal to the protector in him. To make what she wanted to seem noble. He'd rushed to her rescue. He was pathetic.

But he couldn't deny that he wanted her.

He feared he always would.

Abby shifted in his arms, her naked body tangled around his like a vine, her warmth and her scent, a paradise beyond compare.

Never had he opened himself to a woman like he had with Abby. She'd made his fantasies seem pitifully gauche, their lovemaking transcending every experience he'd had to date. Perhaps it was because there was nothing between them. No condom to shield him from her blistering heat, her velvety sheath—a meeting of bodies, a meeting of souls. No so-called protection to stop him from falling for her.

This was a catastrophe.

To reject her now would be callous, besides impossible. To sleep beside her and not feel her in his arms was inconceivable. To know her sadness and not soothe her would have been cold hearted. He'd harboured dreams he had no right to harbour; and now he would pay the price.

He of all people knew the power of thought, the power of suggestion.

He'd brought this woman into his arms as surely as if he'd ordained it. He was the master of his own destiny. Every choice, good or bad, had brought him to this moment. And the price, he feared, would be greater than a pound of flesh. But to feel her, to pleasure her, had been heaven on earth. He savoured the bliss of her curled up against him and tried hard to feel worthy of her.

He was a man borne of violence. She was a woman borne of love.

Hard to see any future there, but for now, he would close his mind to that truth and cherish every moment they shared, knowing, knowing, that walking away from her would be like severing a limb.

"Nico?" Her voice was like silk lingerie, sexy and provocative.

"Mmmmm." He nuzzled into her neck and relished every delicious sensation.

"You helped me conquer my Everest. I owe you so much."

"You owe me nothing. The pleasure was all mine." He'd taken what she'd offered and gorged himself stupid. Gluttony was up there with lust and his sins were mounting by the moment.

Pushing her hair back from her face, he closed his mouth over hers, her heated response detonating new battles, fuelling new surrenders, leaving parts of his soul exposed. He couldn't hide. She filled his head with desires he'd never known. This woman was his. Every stroke of his tongue, every wolfish taste was tainted with his need to possess. To brand her as his. No greater sin than to covet another man's wife... she would belong to someone else in the future. Someone worthy. But right now, she was his and his alone.

Their love making was tender—he wrested his ferocious need for her and what was left was desire. The desire to give her pleasure. The desire to hear his name on her sighs, the desire to commune with his body all that he wanted for her. She deserved to be loved. She deserved to be cherished. She deserved so much more than he had to give, but he gave her everything he had and everything he was. He basked in her languid trust. He revelled in her sensual abandon. He got lost in her touch. And together, they wove promises they couldn't keep.

Every cell in his body was roused by the feel of her—she was an erogenous force he couldn't fight. Every groan, every sigh, every whimper.

He was her knight in shining armour. The man who'd battled the thorns, the wall, the evil enchantment and triumphed. The man who'd freed her from her icy cage.

She was responsive and reactive, and the melding of their bodies was like nuclear fusion or tectonic plates colliding.

He lay wasted and drained of everything except the slamming thud of his heart. Her body lay washed up against him, alive with an answering percussion. His brain was numb, his body shattered. Ravaged from the inside out. Inflamed even now.

No sound from Abby.

No movement.

"Abby, are you okay?" A long pause. He struggled onto his elbow and framed her face with his hand.

"No."

No? He scooped her up against him and held her close, soothing her with his kisses.

Abby's bones were liquid, her body a wasteland. Nico had blasted her into a billion pieces, and she wasn't sure she'd ever feel whole again. Never in her wildest dreams had she imagined sex could be so earth moving. Never in her craziest imaginings had she thought it possible to join with another human being so completely.

This was a treasure indeed.

And it had taken a special man to unlock the wonders of it. Or maybe a practiced one. An experienced one. More rational thoughts started to invade the rosy afterglow. A man who'd scaled the mountain before, who understood the nuances of womanly terrain.

She had to pull herself together. She was twenty-five years old. Old enough to know the difference between reality and fairy tale.

Yet, cradled against him, his arms like bands of steel around her, she felt like a fairy tale princess. Wooed and won. Her heart forever his.

When Abby awoke the next morning, her mind was clear. She slipped away from the shield of Nico's body and left him lazing like a mountain cat in repose.

Retreating to the bathroom, she sought the heavenly pleasure of a hot shower. She ran the soap over her skin and marvelled at how sensitive and reactive it was. Nico had breathed life into her senses. Colours were brighter. Her body was lighter. Her touch was louder.

Her heart was heavier.

No, she wouldn't allow herself to listen to the wishes that whispered at the edge of her awareness. She refused to entertain them for a single moment. She should be celebrating. She was free. Free to be with the man of her choice, safe in the knowledge that she was whole.

Thanks to Nico... who at that moment slipped into the shower recess behind her. His arms wrapped around her and his hands cupped her breasts, gentle and strong, his body hard and earnest against her. His mouth settled hot and slavish against her neck, and she catapulted into fantasy land.

He was good at what he did.

She was oblivious to everything except the hypnotic power of his touch, and when he turned her and lowered his mouth to hers—hungry and devout—she found herself lifted into his arms. Her legs tangled around his waist and he rested her back against the tiles, his hands firmly under her bottom cheeks, his erection hot and eager against that part of her that wanted him most. Her legs tightened around his hips and drew him closer, deeper... and she gave herself up to the wonderful friction as he drove her higher and higher. Their kiss was a greedy, heated tasting, punctuated by sighs and groans and shallow breaths, and her orgasm built fast and furious. She hurtled into paradise, taking Nico with her, their cries melding together.

Abby was slow to recover and how Nico hadn't collapsed beneath her she had no idea. Her own legs were beyond weak and wrapped limply around his waist. She clung to him, nestled against his chest, wet and wild.

He turned so her back was under the heated spray of the

water and reached for the soap. Never had a lathering felt so good. His gentle, careful caress warmed her heart and filled her soul. And when he lowered her feet to the floor, she held on to the broad frame of his shoulders and fought to regain control of her emotions.

"Good morning, or should I say good afternoon." His voice rumbled around the small space, spreading warm syrup through her veins.

"It couldn't be afternoon. Truly?" She lifted incredulous eyes to his, her gaze captured by the blue, blue flame that burned there. "You're very handsome when you're wet." He was drop-dead gorgeous—wet or dry—his eyes, bright and mischievous, his smile… his smile did things to her body that stole the breath from her lungs. His body was macho and scarred, sexy and strong—and how had she kept her hands off him before now? Already, she wanted him again.

"And you're the most sexy woman alive." His voice was husky, and his cheeks dimpled in a way that sent tiny electric shocks all over her body.

Sexy? He knew just what to say to make a girl feel on top of the world. But this was about Nico and what he did to her. She and sexy were poles apart, or at least they had been, until last night… this morning… this afternoon.

"No skiing for us today. We need brunch, maybe a walk, and maybe a talk." His tone was gruff.

"Nico, I'm fine with this. It's all good. It's all better than good. I know the deal."

"You do?"

"I know you don't do commitment. I don't have any false illusions about what you want or what this is."

"Abby, I truly don't know what this is." He raked his hands

through his wet hair, and she knew he was torn between duty and desire.

"Then let me help." He had done so much for her. She would do this for him... she'd put his needs ahead of her own. "I'm yours until we leave this perfect place, and then we walk away. No strings. No promises. No demands."

No strings? Miss Macramé had just offered him a sexual liaison with no strings?

Her proposal was ludicrous, and she was naïve if she thought they could burn up the sheets for the next two weeks and walk away unscathed.

Two weeks of bliss.

Two weeks of heaven.

And he walked away a free man? There was not a chance of that. Already, he craved her. Already, his body yearned for hers like an addict.

"We'll see where this takes us." To purgatory. He lowered his mouth and grazed his lips across the silken softness of hers. He deepened the kiss and tasted with a confidence borne from her fiery reaction to his slightest touch. Here was temptation, and he had no choice but to take what she offered. He wanted what she wanted; she wanted what he wanted, and there was no heeding common sense.

They were both hell-bent on this path to pain.

Chapter Twelve

The road stretched ahead of Raffaele, long and endless, and he found his stride. His headphones played heavy metal rock and his feet pounded the side of the bitumen in time with the beat. He eyed the scenery around him. He liked it here. But he wasn't free to settle down anywhere until he'd repaid his debt to Bruno. They'd find him here as easily as they'd find him anywhere. Besides, Dominico deserved what was coming.

The cold air helped clear his head. Before he'd gone in the slammer, a bottle of scotch would have gone down like lemonade. Prison was one hell of a way to dry out... but the scotch had gone down smooth and dry and parched his decades-long thirst. He'd allowed himself a celebration. Lorenzo was dead, and he had a plan.

The sun shone through the canopy of trees and flashed like a damn siren in his head.

He went over his plan. He looked at it from all angles. He ran with it and considered its strengths and the weaknesses. And then he smirked.

Dominico had fallen for his own fiction. Mr. and Mrs. Bortoli... their marriage was a sham, but that hadn't stopped his brother from taking advantage of his conjugal rights. The listening device had been inspired, and it had been simple enough to slip into the room while the maid was in the bathroom, her trolley in the hallway. He'd just caught the door before it fully closed and waited.

It was like his own personal soap opera. Days of Our Lives... or more accurately, Last Days of our Lives.

And he'd changed his mind. He wasn't going back to prison for anyone. Not even for his brother. This had to look like an accident.

He hadn't booked anything in his own name. Not even the plane ticket. As far as the world knew, he'd been welcomed back into the fold and was bunkered down with his bikie mates. Hadn't he pulled off the perfect kidnapping all those years ago? Hadn't he delivered the woman and the kid as requested? He could hardly be held responsible for his dumb-arse twelve-year-old brother who'd dobbed them into the cops. It was hardly his fault they'd raided the place before the ransom had been paid... and before Bruno had had his fun with the kid.

Raffaele's stomach churned with anticipation, and he dared to picture a small house by the sea, a good distance from the sulphur gas, but walking distance to the local watering hole. Only two bodies stood between him and freedom, Mr. and Mrs. Bortoli. As soon as they were trolleyed out of their hotel room, he'd be free. His debt to Bruno, repaid. His debt to society, repaid. His debt to his brother, repaid.

Nico strode down the hallway towards the small library. The four weeks were nearly up—two more nights and they'd make their way to Bangkok. He'd looked at their travel plans from every angle. This couldn't fail. It was by the far the most dangerous part of the brief—if he didn't count sharing a bed with Abby. He'd lived and breathed Abby Kercher until she was the air he needed to survive.

He'd become used to the nuances of her body and the sound of her pleasure, and his body was enslaved to hers. But what infuriated him most was that the more he'd gotten to know her body, the less he'd gotten to know her.

He was not in the habit of wanting a woman's heart and the slightest whiff of heart usually had him running scared. But, damn it, Abby had taken his on their first night together and shared hers, only to retract the offer and build a wall between them more impenetrable than the Great Divide. He'd given her a glimpse into his childhood—not the worst of it, but more than he'd shared with any woman before. He'd never told the truth about his tattoo. What it represented. *His flight out of hell.*

She was right to keep her distance.

He was desperate to keep his own. He scanned the hotel foyer for danger. Nothing appeared out of order. There were a couple of young girls playing pool on the full-sized billiard table. The couple they'd seen in the drying room the other day were ensconced in the lounge beside the open fire having a heated discussion. An older couple sat near the window reading newspapers and sipping coffee. He released his breath, but he couldn't fight the sense that something was wrong. His stomach was knotted, and the muscles in his shoulders were bunched tight, sending pain into the side of his neck.

He hastened his steps towards the small library, filled with floor to ceiling bookshelves. The air was musty with the smell of old books. He stood back and scanned the titles, but his skin prickled with unease and a chill ran down his spine. He grabbed a book with little heed to which one and left the room.

He needed to get back to Abby. Now.

A loud clanging sound pealed through the hallway and his walk became a run.

"Sorry, sir. This way." One of the porters guided him towards the main entrance. "That's the fire alarm. You'll need to evacuate. Urgently."

Nico pulled away, his jaw clenching. "I need to find my wife."

"I'm sorry, sir. I must insist. You'll have to wait outside."

There was not a chance of that. Nico pushed past the man and ran for the fire stairs. Abby was in their room. Alone. He didn't believe in coincidences and there'd been no mention of a fire drill. He pounded up the concrete steps two at a time and burst through the door onto the top floor. Abby was at the lift, but she turned and ran towards him.

"Abby." The adrenalin drained away and left him as weak as a kitten. She was okay. "Let's take the stairs."

"What is it? There's no smoke." Her hand shook in his.

"I'm not sure. Maybe it's a drill." Not without warning. Not in the middle of the day. He pulled her close to his side and kept his hand on the gun hidden inside his jacket. They raced down the stairs and pushed through the fire escape door into the cold open air. A crowd of guests milled around the car park, their eyes on the windows. There was a light waft of smoke from the North side of the building, the opposite side to their own.

Abby clung to him, her arms tight around his waist, and he pulled her close. His instincts were on high alert, his body tense. He didn't like it. But there'd been no worrying news from the office—beyond Raffaele's release—but there was nothing to suggest he was in New Zealand or that their safety had been compromised.

Five minutes later, a fire truck pulled into the driveway, its sirens blaring, and the firemen rushed into the hotel. Others strode around the building, directing the truck to the far side, where the smoke was nearly gone.

No flames. Nothing to suggest there was any danger.

Nico waited, his breath ratcheting in and out. The scent of Abby's hair pulled at his attention and she snuggled close to stay warm. The air was icy, but the snow that had blanketed the hotel grounds on their arrival had melted away, leaving brown grass and mud.

What the hell was going on?

It turned out a cigarette butt had been dropped into a bin and set fire to the contents, triggering the smoke alarm. Readily contained. He could hear the relief in the voices around him. It seemed like a reasonable explanation.

Abby stepped away and rubbed her hands together. "The Lovely Bones. I haven't read that one, but I'd like to."

Nico had forgotten the book he still held in his hand. He passed it over to Abby and wrapped his arm around her. Their quiet day reading and relaxing, had been a bit more eventful than he would have liked.

They returned to their room and Nico raked the hallway for anything out of the ordinary but could see nothing. He slipped the key card into the lock and Abby headed straight for the bathroom to run a bath.

Nico scanned the suite, his gaze super attentive as it brushed over everything from the rumpled bed in the main bedroom to the couches and coffee table in the lounge area to the small kitchenette and dining area. Nothing seemed out of place. He sat down on the couch by the fire and studied the yellow flames. The suite felt like home, and he'd be sorry to leave.

The food was fabulous, the views stunning and the mountains felt timeless.

He lay back and closed his eyes, his thoughts drifting. It was a smoke-free hotel. How had a cigarette come to start a fire in a bin? What if someone had wanted to create a distraction? For what purpose? The room seemed untouched, but he couldn't know for sure. What if someone had planted a bug? A listening device.

He shot up.

And began to search.

Raffaele looked back at the chateau and grinned. A small fire. Nothing too dangerous. Just enough to create a bit of confusion. It could have been an accident. Someone could have been careless with a sneaky fag and set off the smoke alarm. It had given him enough time to pick the lock to the Te Heu Heu Suite on the top floor and damage the flue. He'd used a screwdriver to split the flue at the join. Luckily, he'd worn gloves because the damn thing had been hot... it must have been going for most of the day. But that was good and would make the process quicker. Even unlit the pilot light would ensure carbon monoxide flowed into the suite. And they'd be asleep or distracted with each other like they'd been every moment since he'd planted the bug. They wouldn't notice the symptoms and they'd be dead by morning. He planned to have breakfast at the chateau, same as he'd done every morning for the past couple of weeks. It was a lovely routine and he'd get front seat viewing when the person who delivered their breakfast found them dead.

Nico combed the suite from one end to the other, and he would have missed it if he hadn't been so determined to find it. The device was tiny and stuck to the under-side of the counter in the guest bathroom. His heart pounded and he cracked the knuckles in his fists. Who'd planted it? How was it possible? They needed to leave. Now.

He increased the volume of the music to cover the sounds of his packing. Was someone watching? He draped a towel over the camera on the smart TV and knocked on the bathroom door. He didn't want to panic Abby, but he needed her to move. He waited in front of the fire, his gaze on the yellow-gold flame, his pulse pounding in his ears.

He couldn't finalise their account without leaving Abby alone and that wasn't going to happen. He'd have to pay later when they got to their alternative accommodation. He'd let down his guard. He'd been distracted. And now Abby was in danger.

They needed to leave… and find a nondescript motel some-where near Auckland until their flight. Their alias had been compromised and their honeymoon was over.

Abby came out of the ensuite looking rosy-cheeked from her bath. She wore grey trackpants and a soft pink cashmere top, and her auburn hair was brushed back into a ponytail. She looked beautiful and his already-racing pulse ratcheted up a notch.

"I'm thinking of a risotto for dinner tonight," she said. "I really loved the mushroom one we had the other day and maybe a glass of Pinot Grigio."

"That sounds delicious. How about a game of billiards and a pre-dinner drink down in the lounge?"

"Sounds great." She frowned as if she'd sensed the incongru-ency between his casual tone and the rigid stance of his body.

He lifted a finger to his mouth and indicated the packed bags on the floor. He strode over and gave her a hug, and with his mouth close to her ear whispered, "Someone planted a bug."

"A spider?" She jumped back and looked around the room.

He'd forgotten her fear of spiders. He pulled her close, feeling the soft crush of her breasts and the pounding thud of her heart against his chest. He waited until the rigidity in her muscles began to ease. "It's fine, honey. I'll get rid of it."

They needed to leave without being seen, which was not so easy when the hotel's windows all faced out towards the front of the building. Anyone would be able to observe them as they made their way to the car... unless he went alone and picked Abby up at the side door, but that would mean leaving her alone which wasn't an option.

He nipped into the bathroom and packed their toiletries, his hands shaking as he zipped the bag closed.

"Did you find it?" The colour had leached from Abby's cheeks.

"Yep, that's one spider you won't have to worry about again."

He lifted her jacket as quietly as he could and handed it to her, his finger on his mouth. She slipped her feet into her runners and he reached into the kitchenette fridge for a couple of bottles of water. "Are you all set?"

"Yep. Let's go. I fully plan to beat you."

"There's two chances of that, hon. Buckley's and None. I grew up in pool halls." He winked and turned to give their suite the once over to make sure he hadn't missed anything. He pulled the door open and used one of their suitcases to hold it while he reached carefully and quietly for the rest.

The riskiest part of his escape plan was now. How to get away without being detected in the late afternoon sun. They took the fire stairs and when he was sure they were alone, he turned to Abby. "There was a listening device in the room. Someone knows we're here. We have to go and now." They reached the ground level, and he pushed the heavy fire escape door open. The car was about two hundred metres away. Whilst there was no one around, the hotel windows meant they were visible to anyone looking in that direction from the guests to the staff to those sitting in the bar or the restaurant downstairs. It was risky but he couldn't see any other option. He felt like a felon—they hadn't paid their account—but his credit card imprint would cover the cost and he'd call later to apologise for their early departure.

"Are you ready?" Abby reached for his hand and squeezed.

"Let's leave the bags here and we'll stroll over to the car. We can come back for them if it's safe."

Nico wrapped his arm around Abby's slender shoulders. He would give his life for this woman, but he hoped that wouldn't be necessary. Their location had been compromised. The words were a roar in his ears. How? His gaze swept the area in front of the hotel. If they could get into their vehicle and disappear before whoever was listening in on their conversations woke up to the fact that they'd gone, they'd be okay… if not?

His palm slipped against Abby's. Despite the brisk breeze coming off the snowy mountains behind the hotel, her hand was sweaty. Probably his, too. With every step he listened, combing the sounds for danger.

One hundred metres.

Fifty.

Ten.

He clicked the automatic lock and opened the door for Abby,

his body between her and anyone approaching from behind him. He closed the door and strolled around the front of the vehicle to join her. His heart banged in his chest and he resisted the urge to look back at the Chateau. So far, so good. He closed the door and swallowed against the lunar landscape of his throat… he reached over and kissed Abby's trembling lips. He started the engine and veered over to where their luggage waited, out of view of any onlookers. He secreted it away in the boot, checked the car for tracking devices and any sign of tampering, and satisfied, sank into his seat. With a wink towards Abby—that belied the adrenalin pounding in his veins—he navigated his way along the driveway, careful to comply with the twenty kilometre an hour speed limit before turning right onto State Highway 48. With his eyes on the rear-view mirror and the empty road behind them, he turned left onto State Highway 47 and pressed his foot to the accelerator.

Raffaele ate his breakfast with his eye on Mt. Ngauruhoe, which rose like a volcanic cone from the flat landscape outside the window. The room was quiet except for the soft murmur of voices, the tinkle of classical music in the background, and the clink of cutlery against porcelain plates. He returned his attention to the pages of the newspaper spread across the table before him and took another bite of the savoury omelette he'd ordered, washing it down with a gulp of quality coffee. His body buzzed with anticipation.

A fire crackled in the huge fireplace and he was glad he'd chosen a table near the large arched window frame. He liked open space. And the scenery here suited him. The stretch of grass before the low-lying trees and the sharp punctuation of the mountain.

The trip had been good for him and seeing his brother, dead, would be the perfect start to his new life. Of course, they could hardly bring the corpses out past the main reception. Why hadn't he thought of that? They'd keep it quiet and wouldn't want the rest of the guests to know what had happened.

He eyed the wait staff.

There was nothing out of the ordinary about their behaviour and he couldn't fathom how they wouldn't be a little more ruffled if guests had been found dead.

A rumour like that would travel like wildfire.

He took another sip of his coffee. Patience was his middle name. Now. In the past he'd lost his temper in the space of a moment, courtesy of his dad's genes—damn it, his hands were shaking. His heart was racing. He had to hold it together. What if the ambulance went around to a side exit? What if the damn thing was there now and he was missing it?

No, he couldn't miss it. Not after all these years.

The police would arrive first. And they'd come in the main entry. He settled back with his coffee, his gaze shifting from the scenery outside, to the lounge area with its chandeliers and striped bucket seats. He didn't know the right name for them. He wasn't an expert in antique furniture or vintage anything, and it seemed the place was full of opulent furnishings and old things.

He drained his coffee and closed the paper. He glanced at his watch. Ten o'clock. Something wasn't right. Well, he could hardly pick the lock, now could he? Nor loiter in the hallway and wait for the maid. Damn it. How could something have gone wrong? He'd used a CO alarm to check the levels and the damn thing had gone off like one of those old-fashioned alarm clocks... the type with bells on the top that near bounced off the bedside table.

Raffaele strolled into the lounge and picked up a billiard cue. He used the plastic triangle to set up a game of pool. *You be large and I'll be small.* When had he started speaking to himself like he was two people? When he'd become his only friend. Prison wasn't a social paradise. He bent forward and whacked the ball with a resounding thud. It bounced off the side cushion and shot straight into the top left pocket. Great shot. He circled the table and lined up another.

And another.

And still there was no damn sign of any coppers. Just the word lifted the follicles of his skin. He'd take a wander and hope his hiking gear was enough to make him invisible. He was a loner. A walker. And a quick pace around the outside of the chateau told him something was very wrong.

Chapter Thirteen

"How far is it to the airport?"

Abby looked at Nico and he was blown away by how effective the disguise was. She looked like a man with padding placed carefully around her waist to make her look overweight and to draw attention away from her... he gulped ...breasts. The thought was akin to calling the demons inside him to rise and salute. She sported loose clothing and a mousy moustache and beard. Her hair was up inside her cap. She wore small wire-framed glasses and a frown that wouldn't have looked out of place on a true down-and-out criminal.

"About twenty minutes."

Two nights in an ammonium scented, out-of-date Auckland motel and they'd outrun the trouble that had found them. The thought was like acid or a third-degree burn. Abby was safe. They had a new rental car and their compromised identities—Mr. and Mrs. Bortoli—were long gone. Even now, his breath caught in his throat and his body felt like he'd stepped on a live landmine.

Nico kept his eyes on the road. It was early, and the traffic was sparse. "We have a long day ahead. Our flight to Melbourne leaves in..." He glanced at his watch. "...two hours. Our flight to Bangkok should arrive around midnight

Bangkok time."

The trial would begin the next morning. The part of his plan that stressed him the most was his reliance on the Thai police. But he'd stay close. He'd promised to get Abby to the trial safely and that's what he would do. Little had he known how much his promise would cost him.

"Nico?"

"Yep?" They'd become stupidly formal over the past two days as if the formality could protect them from an intimacy that had grown a life of its own. No longer would he wake beside her. No longer would their passion burn into the wee hours of the morning. No longer were his rings on her finger. Miss Macramé had kept her word. No knots to be seen. No strings. What had happened on the mountain... stayed on the mountain.

He hadn't agreed to the stupid deal in the first place.

"Thank you... for keeping me safe." She took a sip of her takeaway coffee.

Was that a hitch in her breath?

"We're not done and dusted yet." She could take that any way she liked and as he said the words, he recognised the truth in them. He didn't do commitment. He didn't do marriage. He didn't believe in it—love turned to hate. But his heart would always belong to Abby. Not that she wanted it. She'd made that clear enough. No other woman had come close to Abby. No other woman could.

"The hardest part is still to come. We'll arrive in Bangkok, hours before the trial starts. You'll be taken into custody by the Thai police and spend what's left of the night at the prison hospital. They'll deliver you to the courthouse first thing the next morning."

"I trust you completely."

Not enough to give him her heart.

He didn't want her heart. He didn't do hearts. He had to get a grip. Her deal was a ball-breaker, but she'd been right to protect herself. And he should have been the one doing the protecting. Wanting more than he had a right to ask for was failing her in the extreme. *Toughen up. The woman needs a man to keep her safe, not a mouse musketeer.*

"The best-laid plans can go awry." He couldn't afford to be off his game. He had a job to do. First, he'd keep her alive and help her to put those lowlifes behind bars, then he'd lick his wounds and try to figure out how he was going to breathe without her.

Her face twisted away like she couldn't bear to look at him now that the deal was done. Anger curled somewhere deep inside him. The precious princess was back, and he'd never felt more churlish. It was too damned late. He should never have allowed her to get close in the first place. He'd known the dangers going in even if she hadn't. Not that he'd had any choice. She'd blasted her way into his heart and taken no prisoners.

He reached for his coffee and took a gulp, the liquid burning him all the way to his stomach.

Abby appeared polite and aloof, cool, and unreadable. His life had changed irrevocably. He wasn't the same person he'd been. She'd changed him. He'd disintegrated in her arms and she'd put him back together in a different way.

He was wired to want her.

She on the other hand had shed the woman she'd become in his arms like a snake shed its skin. The woman beside him right now was the same woman who'd sat beside him on the way to Mt. Ruapehu. Self-contained. Brave. A warrior woman with no need for a knight in not-so-shiny armour.

He got it. He just didn't like it. Temper took the reins, and he contained the power of it, just. He shoved the cardboard coffee cup back into its place in the console.

"How long will the flight take from Melbourne to Bangkok?" Abby's mind was on practicalities like his should be.

"Fourteen and a half hours." Too long to be near her and not touch her. He wanted to go back in time to their mountain hideaway with its fickle temperament.

Stop. This had to stop. He just had to let her go. Get his mind off Abby and onto the main game.

"Melbourne is two hours behind Auckland and three hours ahead of Bangkok."

He forced his gaze back on the road. Off the woman. Onto the job ahead. "It might be wise to sleep on the plane if you can. We're taking commercial flights this time in economy. We won't have much time for sleep once we get to Bangkok."

"I don't imagine my kind of man would fly first class."

"No." Hell. Hours and hours crammed into a seat so close together their legs would touch. He hadn't thought this through very well at all. He reached for his coffee. "And we'll be handcuffed together for the duration of the flight."

"You're joking?" Her eyes flashed and there was no missing the Abby he knew and loved.

With his gaze back on the road, he took a sip of his coffee. "No."

"There's not a chance you're coming into the bathroom with me."

"It's a bit late to be self-conscious don't you think?"

"Some things should stay private."

He'd got to her. He could see that in the jut of her chin. Good. Anything was better than the cool serenity she wore like a mask. "Not long now and you can put all of this behind you." He couldn't stop the bitterness from seeping into his tone.

He'd never begged a woman to be with him, and he wasn't going to start now. Besides, he knew the magic didn't last forever. He should feel relieved. He could get back to his work. He hadn't thought trades or currencies in weeks. Never had he lost his focus so completely.

But far from rejuvenated, he felt gutted.

The handcuff cut into Abby's skin, metal against bone, leaving her wrist red and sore.

People stared.

The contrast between her and Nico couldn't have been more dramatic. Nico looked ravishing in a dark suit and aviator sunglasses—all dark-angel sexy—and she was a scruffy disgrace, shuffling beside him, her wrist handcuffed to his.

Nico giveth and Nico taketh away.

From feeling like the sexiest woman on the planet, she'd sunk to a new kind of low. No chance he'd find her anything but resistible now. In her saggy jeans and bogan flannelette shirt, she was about as attractive as a tradie's bum crack. This was how he'd remember her. Hairy, repulsive, and overweight. Fabulous. She felt like baring her teeth at those who stared at them.

Worse, she was attached to Nico—by the wrist! He could feel every tell-tale lurch in her pulse when their thighs brushed. He would know that he got to her.

The one thing she'd demanded of herself—to walk

away—had become the biggest challenge of her life. Far greater than the trial. Far greater than standing on her own two feet.

Yet here they were, and it was a reality she'd have to live with.

She'd be chained to him forever, one way or another. The cuffs mocked her resolution to keep him at a safe distance. How was that possible when he'd become a part of her?

This was about his experience and her lack of it. He walked away from this kind of thing *all the time*. The article she'd read about him was etched into her memory. Foolhardy indeed, to fall for a man who sauntered from one conquest to the next, with a swagger and a notch in his belt.

He was her bodyguard. He'd warned her of just this kind of danger. Misinterpreting fear as passion, reliance as need, relief as love. Forewarned was forearmed except it wasn't working.

She wanted, she needed, she loved.

Damn the man to Hades. He'd taken her to heaven, only to leave her in hell. In Bangkok, he'd relinquish his responsibility. With his promise to her father fulfilled, he'd walk away.

She'd known the price going in. No demands. She wasn't the type to break her promise. He'd done so much for her. She of all people knew there was no such thing as something for nothing. Everything had its price. Everyone had their price.

Heaven came at one hell of a price.

There were some things that neither Nico nor her father could protect her from. Like the walk of shame through the airport.

Taken onto the plane before everyone else, she and Nico settled into their seats. The flight steward could scarcely conceal his distaste. What had they been told? What had she done? What kind of criminal was she? Why hadn't she thought to ask?

As soon as the steward was out of earshot, she whispered the words, her tone waspish. "What the hell did I do to deserve that kind of look?"

"You murdered a man. A drug deal gone bad."

"What? Are you insane?" She was a murderer?

"It's a story, Abby, keep it together. How else could I justify the tight security?"

Oh, this day was going from bad to worse; from worse to intolerable. She still had to get through two flights attached to a man who couldn't wait to get unattached and leave her to her future. A future without him. Perhaps the cure was worse than the condition. At least before, she hadn't known what she was missing. Now, she knew it through to her bones. He'd ruined her for any other man. Pampered. Princess. The words whispered in her ears.

She'd promised she'd walk away and walk away she would. To put the onus on Nico would be poor form indeed after all that he'd done for her. She steeled every aching part of herself. She wanted more. She craved more. She couldn't have more.

And there was the trial to get through.

The plane filled with people and Abby settled her gaze on the window, her vision blurring. The plane taxied along the runway and still she struggled to regain control.

The conditions had been clear going in. She'd known there would be a cost. It wasn't like he'd wooed her with false promises. The only promise going in was that she'd let him go when their time was up.

Except she wanted to hold on and never let him go. She fisted her free hand against the deep throb inside her. The only place she wanted to be was in his arms. The only place she felt safe was by his side.

But she was a fat, slovenly, despicable lawbreaker of the wrong gender... and that told her something about the way he planned to manage any residual attraction. What she needed to do was visualise him as something other than a dark, avenging angel.

Raffaele arrived at the airport at first light. The previous day had been fruitless. No sign of his brother or his whore. How they'd survived was beyond him. He'd entered the room in the wake of the maid and seen with his own two eyes that their belongings were gone. He'd left a message at the hotel from Mr. Bortoli complaining about the yellow flame and the risks of carbon monoxide poisoning, along with an urgent request to get the flue checked. He wouldn't be responsible for anyone else dying in that suite.

How had Dominico guessed?

Raffaele had a ticket for the last flight to Bangkok and he settled into a seat at the food court with a coffee and a newspaper. Failure was not an option. They had to be here somewhere. He would cross paths with them sooner or later... and when he did? He touched his hand luggage and the handle he'd sharpened into a blade. No way could he have missed them. He'd observed every single passenger waiting for a flight to anywhere... there was the slim chance they'd headed directly to the airport when they'd left the hotel, but plane tickets weren't that easy to rearrange at short notice.

His brother was wily enough to take a circuitous route, but Raffaele had staked out the airport. He would have seen them, no matter the flight.

He waited until the final boarding call, and with a forced smile and an apology to the stewardess, made his way down the centre aisle, his breath coming in puffs and pants. He skimmed every passenger on the plane. Nothing. By the time he reached his allocated seat he was ready to kill every damn one of them. How had Dominico gotten his whore out of the country without Raffaele seeing them? It wasn't like the chit was hard to recognise.

And then it struck him. Of course, a disguise. An older woman? A grey wig. A walking stick. A geriatric couple?

His hatred for his brother was coloured with pride.

The plane hurtled along the Melbourne tarmac and bulleted into the sky. Thrust back against her seat, Abby fought her emotions, her mind oblivious to the roar of the engines. By the time the plane levelled out, she had a precarious hold on them.

"Are you okay?"

"Yes." She lied.

Nico reached into his bag and pulled out a novel. "Would you like something to read?"

"Sure. Thank you."

The title was a blur. She could no more focus on the text than she could calm the rapid beat of her heart. Her chest felt tight and every breath brought another wave of darkness. The disguise was essential to her safety. She had a job to do before she could fall apart and feel miserable. Stay strong. Keep her eye on what was important. Like making sure these thugs stayed behind bars. Her testimony was important. For the children they'd exploited. For Gary. And his mates.

Nico reached across and closed the book that lay unread

on her lap. He ripped the plastic from a set of headphones. "Maybe you'd prefer to watch a movie?"

"Okay." Abby went through the motions and selected a movie she'd once wanted to see. A romantic comedy. Too chick flick for the man she was?

Nico's gaze was never far away, the blue heat of it like a smouldering burn against her skin. Her mind swarmed with remembered sensations. His strength. His vulnerability. His tattoo—the black bird that represented his flight out of darkness. His freedom from the past. But he was chained to his past like a raptor to its trainer—unaware of its talons, its sharp beak, its potential to shred its captor into a bloody pulp. The air between them sparked with tension, and when the back of his hand pressed against hers, her body reared away. Damn him. Didn't he know how hard this was? She scowled in his direction, her mood more befitting the criminal in his charge than the pampered princess she used to be.

"You have only yourself to blame." His tone was gentle, but his gaze was ragged.

"I'm well aware of that." She swallowed against the raw knot in her throat. "Don't worry, I'm tougher than you think." Tough? She'd never felt weaker. Almost every word that came out of her mouth was a lie. She couldn't tell him the truth. Not when he didn't want to hear it. Not when he'd done so much.

"Are you sure about that?" The timbre of his voice was like a burr under her skin.

"I'm tough enough." Tough enough to leave you. Tough enough to keep my word. Had he guessed that she loved him? That to leave him would be like cutting out her heart. Was he concerned she wouldn't be able to hold it together for the trial? Did he think she'd be a liability? The thought was an unpalatable one.

His eyebrow lifted and she refused to give him the satisfaction of knowing he was right. "Thank you… for looking out for me." Lovely to see you again didn't come close to describing how earth shifting their reunion had been. Nor would it befit the sullen lawbreaker she'd become. Abby held his gaze for a short moment before shifting her focus back to the screen. She started the movie and like the pathetic addict she was, she savoured his closeness for their last precious hours.

And after the trial, she'd grit her teeth and walk away. As promised.

Chapter Fourteen

Nico unlocked the cuff around his wrist and clicked it into place on the wrist of the Thai police officer. They were in a small room off the main customs area. He'd had the fellow's history checked to the nth degree. No corruption charges. No dirty dealing. He'd come highly recommended, but that didn't mean he was clean.

"You will protect this man with your life." Nico's voice was low and no-nonsense. Abby stood broken, her gaze on the floor.

"Yes, sir." The man's English was heavily accented. He was the only officer in the security contingent aware of their cargo's true identity. The rest believed they'd taken custody of a despicable felon, and Nico didn't want her manhandled.

"I'll be watching." Nico indicated to his eyes.

"Yes, sir." The man's gaze was respectful. "No problem."

Nico could discern nothing but humility. "Good." This was the riskiest part of his plan and now that they were here, every cell in his body objected. To hand her over into someone else's care was counter intuitive. He'd rather see her to the trial himself, but this was the safest option. This was outside the square. He had to think unpredictable.

Abby's gaze was sullen and lack-lustre. She pulled off the

disguise to perfection. He watched her scuff away, surrounded by armed officers, and it was the single most difficult thing he'd ever had to do. He couldn't afford to be worried. He needed to focus. He strode down the hallway in their wake, his gaze alert for anything suspicious.

The officer had given him a small electronic communication device so he could remain in contact. Abby drew attention, but not the sort he'd feared. He pulled their suitcases behind him and followed the group out of the air-conditioned building. The air was hot and thick and humid despite the late hour.

Abby was shoved into the back of a police van and several officers accompanied her. Nico was on hyperalert, adrenalin coursing through his veins. His staff had organised a small hire car for Nico to use and he was relieved to see it parked behind a police vehicle. So far, so good.

He piled the suitcases into the back and lowered himself into the driver's seat. He quickly familiarised himself with the layout and turned the key. He checked the roadway was clear and moved into the traffic, separated from Abby by one vehicle.

Darkness engulfed him as soon as he left the busy hub of the airport. The highway wasn't well lit and Nico's stress levels rocketed. He paid scant attention to the shadowy roadside scenery during the thirty-or-so minute drive, his attention glued to the van.

What was going on inside?

Nico gritted his teeth against his fear. What if the operation had been compromised and the men who wanted her dead were dressed as officers? They could have killed her, and he'd be none the wiser. No, she was cuffed to a reliable man.

His grip on the steering wheel slipped and slid. Perspiration slid down his forehead and he swiped it away. The window was down, but the hot air did little to relieve his discomfort.

He needed to focus. Never get involved with the person you're protecting. It was simple. Rules were there for a reason. Clear mindedness was essential. His head was a melting pot of emotions and sensations. How could he have thought this would work? How could he have entrusted her safety to anyone else?

No one else had as much to lose if this went wrong.

He pushed the thought away and overtook a car that sat between them. His breath was shallow and choppy, and he couldn't fill his lungs despite his best efforts to do so. He steadied his gaze on the dark red Thai number plate in front of him. It had a white police logo and five digits—19422. It was battered and unkempt, like the vehicle itself.

Their arrival at Bang Kwang Central prison couldn't come soon enough. His hands had fused with the steering wheel, and the white bones of his knuckles gleamed under the muted light. He had to prise his fingers off one at a time. His gaze raked the scene for danger, his body rigid.

The back of the van opened, and the police descended. Where was she? His eyes cut through the night. There. Her gaze snagged on his for a breathless moment before she was pushed towards the entry. Her feet stumbled and adrenalin shot into his veins. He was out of the car in the blink of an eye.

This woman mattered to him. That fact had been rammed home with the force of a battering iron. She'd given herself to him in every possible way, then closed her heart to him like he'd trespassed on sacred soil. Damn her. He wanted her still. Far from sating his desire, she'd stoked it. She was forged of tougher stuff than he could have guessed. And she'd kept her promise… But what if he wanted the damn strings? The thought stalled his forward motion and his foot hovered in mid-air like he was a marionette and the puppeteer had forgotten to propel him.

Love scared him more than the very real possibility he was in the sights of a weapon. He swallowed hard against the rising bile.

He had a job to do and he planned to do it. He wanted her alive and free to live her life—then he'd walk away even if it killed him.

Love today was violence tomorrow.

Violence was in his blood and if he loved Abby, the best thing he could do was step back and allow her to find a man who was worthy of her, if any such man existed.

Leg irons?

Abby bit hard against the pain and the shame as she was shackled like a common criminal. Prison life in Thailand was no garden picnic and her only consolation was the knowledge that she had the power to keep the men who'd torn her world apart in just this position. She'd been forced to change into government-issue shorts and a t-shirt, and her feet were bare.

The shackles around her ankles were heavy and cumbersome and she couldn't move freely. The other officers peeled away as Nico's man ferried her towards the medical unit. He pointed to the bathroom in the corner of the room and settled her onto a bed, pulling the curtains around it. He unlocked the shackles and the cuffs but left them nearby. "We'll put these back on in the morning. I'll be right outside if you need me. You're safe here. There's biscuits or fruit if you're hungry, and water." He pointed to a bottle of water and a glass on the set of drawers next to the bed.

Abby lay back and tried to sleep, but the facial hair glued to her skin was intolerably itchy. There was the low hum of a ceiling fan, and the slow flow of air around her. With only a few hours until morning, she needed to rest.

For the first time, she lost her nerve, realising just how dangerous her situation was. In New Zealand, the trial had seemed so far away and the dangers, surreal. Now? Tears welled in her eyes. She had to hold it together. Her friends had died, and she had lived.

And now thanks to Nico, she would testify, and those bastards would rot in prison for a very long time. He'd kept her safe. As safe as she could be—in a Thai prison. Points to Nico for doing the unexpected.

And he'd taught her more about passion in the past three weeks than she'd dreamed possible. She couldn't get him out of her head. Every thought was of Nico. Her body ached, craved, and hankered for him.

Abby woke to the glare of artificial light. She shielded her eyes and struggled to her feet. She gulped down some water and visited the bathroom. The officer waited a polite distance away and when she was ready, he shackled her feet and cuffed her wrist to his.

Once they were out in the passageway, she was surrounded by guards and a volley of words in Thai that she couldn't understand. One of them shoved her ahead of him.

Images flashed into her mind of her mother screaming. Of a rough hand covering her mother's mouth, her eyes wide and terrified. Of a man hurting her.

Of her own fear. Of a rough hand clamped over her mouth, her teeth crushed into her lip. Of her struggle to breathe.

Not real. Her father's words echoed in her mind. A bad dream... the bad dream from her childhood.

She was safe. Nico would protect her. This was part of his plan... and she had to trust him. He'd promised her father if nothing else.

Where was he? Had he already gone back to his life in Sydney? The thought pierced her heart like an arrow, and she staggered, stubbing her bare toe on the concrete. A beat-up prison bus waited outside the building. The sun was low in the sky, but the air was humid, and her clothing stuck to her body. With her free hand, she swiped at her brow and scratched at the hair on her face. In the short moment between leaving the building and being pushed into the back of the vehicle, she took a deep breath of the morning air, the sweet fragrance of jasmine counterposed by the ripe undertone of sewage. She sank onto a hard bench in the back of the vehicle and nearly choked on the stench of stale perspiration.

The erratic drive to the courthouse was short and her arrival unheralded. No press, no cameras, no drama. It was like she was invisible. Invisible was good, wasn't it?

Anger fought with her fear, and grit wrestled her weakness. She could do this. She would do this. She had to do this. For Gary and his mates. For the children. For herself.

Nico's plan unfolded around her and she found herself infused with courage.

Nico watched as the prison bus made its way past the main entrance to the Bangkok Criminal Court at the north end of the court complex. He leaned against an enormous banyan tree in Ratchada Road, on a bend known as the curve of a hundred corpses. He looked like a western tourist-bum with his cheap summery shirt, dark sunglasses and a camera strapped over his shoulder. His legs were tanned despite the winter hiatus and he wore khaki shorts and thongs. He sipped an iced coffee and watched, every muscle on alert. He observed the guards in their dark grey uniforms and berets at the entrance but didn't breathe easily until the vehicle carrying Abby had turned safely off the main road and moved towards the rear of the building.

His gaze shifted back to the main entry—a grand portico with Thai lettering in gold, and columns that looked like oversized prison bars. Abby had arrived. She was safe. The adrenalin rushed out of his body, leaving him limp—as limp as the Thai flag that hung motionless above the portico. There was no breeze, nothing to cool the beading of sweat on his forehead. The night had been warm with no relief from the oppressive humidity.

He turned his attention to his bacon and egg McMuffin and relaxed back against the tree's solid trunk.

If his eyes hadn't been on the entrance, he might not have seen the lone officer in a khaki-coloured Thai police uniform.

And if he hadn't been the man he was, he might not have appreciated the difference between this guy and the shorter Thai officers who had met them at the airport. His walk was jaunty, almost cocky. He was muscular and solid. Olive-skinned. Dark sunglasses. But it was his jawline—shadowed with dark growth—that had Nico lowering his food. The fellow nodded to the guards and made his way up the bank of stairs. He stopped at the top and turned, his gaze sweeping behind him and along the length of the road, before zeroing in on Nico where he stood beneath the shelter of the banyan tree. Nico's body reacted like someone had run a live wire over his skin.

Recognition struck him like a pistol whip.

Raffaele looked older and the week-old scruff on his face made it harder to identify him, but the way he held his body, the gorilla-like curve of his shoulders, the way his hands curled into fists even at rest, the black energy that emanated from him... Nico's breakfast stirred in his stomach. His brother was here, in Bangkok, at the courthouse.

And if Raffaele had done his homework, he'd have known that Thai police officers were clean-shaven. No way had he come by that uniform honestly. He was likely racking up misdemeanours faster than tourists could snap up counterfeit watches.

Nico lifted his iced coffee to his lips to cover his face, his gaze taking in the pistol on his brother's belt. His concern was fast followed by fear. Fear for Abby. And fear for Raffaele. What had he gotten himself into this time?

His brother turned and disappeared through the doorway.

Nico moved fast, dropping his unfinished breakfast in a nearby bin. He spoke into his earpiece and warned the officer who had accompanied Abby. He hoped his curious tourist ruse would be enough to get him inside the courthouse. He ran towards the building with its row of shady palms and grassy verge, his thongs slapping against the roadway. His breath came hard and fast, and as he scaled the stairs, he fought to settle it. He nodded to the security guards at the top and slipped past them into the air-conditioned cool of the foyer. His first thought was relief, fast followed by strategic consideration of the space around him. No sign of Raffaele.

Abby was on the first floor in a cell used for detaining suspects, and his contact would make sure she was protected. He glanced around as a tourist might, taking a photo here and there. His casual stroll belied the bow-taut tension in his body. He tucked his thongs into his back pocket and wandered in bare feet.

Where the hell was Raffaele?

Raffaele could see the appeal. The Royal Thai Police uniform made him feel powerful and he puffed out his chest. He hoped the dark sunglasses and police-issue peaked cap with its metal badge were enough to hide the fact that he wasn't Thai. He thought he looked the part, although he'd sensed a slight hesitation in the security guards at the gate. He'd lay low and wait until Abby and Nico showed up. The guise had gotten him into the building—with a pistol.

He made his way to the eighth floor and strode along the passageway towards the relevant court room. He was high up... higher than the palm trees that grew in a neat row below. He observed the bank of windows, the catch that allowed each one to open. This had to go well. If he failed? He assessed the distance to the ground. He was a dead man. One way or another. Bruno wasn't the forgiving kind.

He felt a soft gust of cool air and his gaze lifted to the air-conditioning vent in the ceiling above his head. Of course. He could navigate the air-conditioning system. Two shots from above and in the confusion, no one would know where they'd come from. Then he'd navigate his way to a safe place—a men's bathroom—and leave the building the same way he'd come in. In plain view. Yes. He eyed the vent near the entrance to the courtroom. Was there a side entrance? No. This was the only way in except for the doors at the front of the courtroom that led to the judge's chambers.

He would see Abby and Dominico arrive.

And then they'd die.

Nico's body was wired like an electric charge. There was no sign of Raffaele. None. Had he been mistaken? No. His heartbeat pounded, and his brow dripped. Salty perspiration stung his eyes.

With his breath hogtied in his lungs, he listened, sifting through the sounds around him. There were the guards at the entry, the foreign timbre of the Thai language. And the tinny sound of traditional Thai music that came through the building's sound system. He settled his gaze on a glass framed document, but in truth, he scoped the area reflected behind him. It was an enormous building and Raffaele could be anywhere.

But Abby's case would be heard in a courtroom on the eighth floor and if what he suspected was true, then his brother would be lurking there. Had Raffaele tracked them to New Zealand? Was he responsible for the listening device that Nico had found in their room at the Chateau Tongariro?

But why? To seek retribution against the younger brother who'd dobbed him in? And if so, why hadn't he confronted him in New Zealand? Why had he come to Bangkok? How could he have known they were coming here?

Nico moved to the stairwell and began the arduous climb. When he got to the eighth floor, his breath came fast from tight lungs, but the passageway was empty. There was a bank of windows with a ledge outside, accessible from the inside. Good to know.

The courtroom walls were lined with timber. A huge wooden bench spanned much of the space at the front of the room and three black leather chairs waited behind it. Nico scanned the rows of empty wooden seats on either side of the central passage and eyed the stationary ceiling fans. Raffaele would have to hide in clear view and what better disguise than that of a police officer?

Smart. Not a word he'd usually use when he thought of his brother.

Nico could warn the authorities that there was a man impersonating a police officer... but he was no longer a twelve-year-old kid, and he knew the dangers of the Thai prison system. Did he really want his brother to starve in an overcrowded Bangkok prison cell?

His instinct was to protect Raffaele, but what if his brother shot Abby in cold blood? His own blood ran cold, and he spoke into his communication device. They needed to access the security footage around the court room and figure out what his brother had in mind.

Raffaele watched Dominico from the vent system in the ceiling, his pistol poised to blast a bullet into his chest. His finger itched to pull the trigger, but to kill his brother now would ruin his plans for the girl. No. Two shots. Two deaths. Two hours to wait.

Abby stood under the hot water and scrubbed her body with soap. Her ankles and wrists burned, where they'd been rubbed by the metal shackles and cuffs. She squirted a generous pool of shampoo into her palm and lathered it into her hair. Tears mingled with the water and she fought to pull herself together.

The lure of coffee drew her out of the water and into the protective vest, silk shirt and fitted skirt that had been arranged for her to wear. It seemed Nico was destined to buy her underwear. The thought had her heart racing and falling at the same time, her mood more oppressive than the heat outside.

He'd left her. In good hands. Looked after. Alone.

She sat at the wooden table in the empty room in silence, except for the quiet whir of the ceiling fan above. She lifted the cover from a bowl to find a spice-scented broth with rice and vegetables. She reached for the spoon like an automaton and ate mechanically... forcing herself to swallow. Her gaze slipped from the stained cabinets and counter to the pinboard on the wall near the door. Papers fluttered in the breeze—their corners curled in towards the centre. She, too, felt flat and curled in, like she'd been unable to wash away her fake persona. She reached for her coffee and took hold of the chipped mug. The rich scent roused her, and she sipped. And she remembered she wasn't alone. The police officer Nico had trusted to protect her was on the other side of the door.

There was a hollow knock and Abby jumped like she'd been hit by a two hundred and forty volt current. Not Nico. A Thai woman. A nurse? Her melancholy resettled around her, but she forced herself to smile. She offered up her broken skin to be tended to and expressed her thanks.

The officer appeared in the doorway and nodded. It was time. Abby rose to her feet and followed him along the passageway. She should have felt safe surrounded by security staff, but there was no sign of Nico and instead, she felt angsty and unsettled. And when they arrived on the eighth floor, it was hot and sticky. Was there something wrong with the air-conditioning? Someone had opened several windows in the hope of a breeze, but after twenty steps down the hallway, the protective vest under her shirt had stuck to her skin and sweat beaded on her forehead. At least the heat took her mind off her fear. She had to have faith. In Nico. In herself. And she trusted him to protect her person even if she couldn't trust him with her heart.

And then they were outside the courtroom.

A man balanced on an A-frame ladder, the top half of his body in the air conditioning duct, hopefully remedying the problem. He wore khaki shorts... and then her pulse pounded hard in her chest. She'd know those legs anywhere. Nico was here?

For the briefest moment, the rush of adrenalin eased and the awful tangle inside her released. Breathe. She lifted her chin and faced forward. She needed to get the job done and put this behind her. Put him behind her.

There was the ear-piercing sound of a gunshot and Abby landed hard and heavy on the floor, a weight forcing the air from her lungs. She lay rigid and still. *Don't move.* Memories rose like ghouls. Gary's body on hers. The warm rush of his blood as his life drained way. The terror of being found. *Hush. Don't make a sound. Don't scream. Don't cry. Don't beg...*

Another shot.

And screams. Yells to stay down. There was the taste of blood in her mouth where her tooth had pierced her lip. The smell of perspiration... she couldn't breathe.

Running feet.

A dreadful scream.

And for a dreadful nanosecond... silence. Then the crushing weight lifted, and she gulped the warm air. Someone pulled her to her feet—her useless feet. The solid presence of the officer who'd looked after her. Nico's voice. "Get her into the courtroom!"

Her body shook like a wobbly jelly and her tears were bitter.

She would testify against these bastards if it killed her, which it nearly had. At least this time the man who'd thrown himself on top of her, prioritising her life over his own, had survived. She sat on a wooden bench and when she finally caught her breath, she noticed the ladder outside the doorway that lay on its side. There was chaos. People down. People dead? Was Nico hurt? She'd heard his voice… he was okay. He had to be okay.

Nico stood at the window and looked down at the uniformed body sprawled on the pavement below. He couldn't believe Raffaele had done it. His neck was at an awful angle and Nico knew he was dead. He'd tried to stop him. He'd called his name and Raffaele had turned towards him, his blue eyes locking with Nico's—and then he'd jumped. Nico would go to his grave with the sound of his brother's scream in his ears.

His chest ached from where the bullet had thwacked into his vest. His brother had taken a shot at him. His brother had tried to kill him. And he'd tried to kill Abby. One of Abby's security detail was down—temporarily—winded by a bullet. Another had a graze across his shoulder. But Abby was safe. Abby was alive.

Nico's hatred for his brother pulsed with a life of its own. His black blood raced thick and furious in his veins. He raked back his sweat-drenched hair and waited for the police and ambulance to arrive.

His own brother had tried to kill them. Yet another secret to add to the hot, stinking pile that rose between he and Abby like an impenetrable wall.

Chapter Fifteen

Abby left the courthouse in the garb of a catholic nun and settled in a nondescript vehicle beside her security detail, who were dressed as priests. She'd testified and gotten justice for Gary and the others, and for the innocent children abused by those despicable men. And she'd sat before the three judges, her face wet with tears, her body soaked with sweat from the protective vest and the heat. She'd had a long shower afterwards, which had helped her to revive, but she felt as fragile as a child.

There was no sign of Nico beyond the unfolding events which communicated to her loud and clear that her safety was his number one priority. He'd delivered her safely to the trial—and he'd deliver her safely home. As promised. But her heart was shattered.

A car horn blared to their right, and Abby jumped, her instinct to pull into herself and make herself small. Adrenalin shot into her veins and stole her strength. The car swerved, and she clung to the seat, her grip slippery from the sheen of sweat on her palms. She despised the jittery sensation inside her… her need to scan the roadside for danger.

She arrived safely at the airport and her breath lost its grabby feel. Her priestly security detail surrounded her. One behind and one on each side.

It seemed like the airport concourse was full of couples. One couple meandered right in front of them—hand in hand—their laughter scraping over Abby's skin like broken fingernails. Another couple pulled matching hand-luggage, their free arm around each other. Abby felt like she was wearing boots of concrete.

She had priority boarding and once she was seated, her detail stepped away and left her in peace. A business-class seat this time. Her gaze clung to the window. Heat shimmered off the tarmac and a row of palm trees skirted the massive building that housed the impressively modern facility. She sat with her hands clasped together—in truth to settle the shaking she couldn't control—but in a manner befitting a bride-of-Christ.

Where was Nico? She might be safe, but disappointment lodged under her ribs like a blade. He hadn't met her at the airport. He hadn't sought her out after the trial. He'd left her to return to Sydney alone. She wouldn't see him again. The thought stabbed at her like a knife.

Her father would be anxious to see her before she travelled back to Melbourne, and her mother... Abby's stomach clenched. She refused to live in fear. Never would she lock herself away from the world like her mother had. It didn't count that her mother's prison was a harbour-side mansion with twenty-first century technology that brought the outside world in. She lived in a gilded cage.

But was Abby's life any better?

Sure, she'd ventured out into the world and found a job—a job that mattered—but now she had the uncomfortable realisation that she was afraid of needing anybody. She stood *alone*. That was how she liked it.

But after being with Nico? Her old life seemed more desolate than her mother's.

Tears welled in her eyes and the image outside the window blurred and multiplied. She wanted Nico. She wanted his arms around her. She wanted him to care about her as much as she cared about him.

She didn't care about him.

The only person she cared about was herself. She was a spoilt daddy's girl. A pampered princess. His words of five years ago pricked at her and she steeled her spine.

She missed his touch. That hardly counted as love. It was the worst kind of naivety to think she loved him. She desired him. She wanted him. She was in lust.

Her body throbbed. Her heart hurt. Her head ranted. The truth was—no matter how hard she tried to reason it away—she loved him.

It was the worst kind of stupidity to fall in love with a man who left a trail of women like human debris in his wake. She'd known that going in. She'd closed her heart and locked it away to keep it safe. Except he'd blasted those locks apart like they didn't exist. He'd filled her heart with his worshipping touch and seduced her mind with his intelligence and he'd cared about her safety. He'd built a wall to protect her virtue.

It wasn't a rational feeling.

It wasn't something she could control. She didn't want to love him. Loving him was never part of the deal. She'd wanted liberation, not captivation.

How had it all gone so wrong?

A stewardess interrupted her reverie to offer her a glass of champagne. Did nuns drink champagne? She couldn't imagine it.

"No, thank you." She tried to smile. Tried to remember the person she'd been before she'd become the person who couldn't breathe without Nico. She turned her attention back to the window and the tarmac and the planes and the zooming luggage carts. Tears welled in her eyes and clung to her lashes.

She'd been through an ordeal. But the ordeal of the trial had been overshadowed by the ordeal of leaving Nico. She wanted to know more about what had happened to him as a child. Like how he'd gotten those scars? She knew his father was abusive and those marks had been put there by the man entrusted with his care.

Nico's rejection of her was grounded in envy. Her father loved and pampered her, while his father had hurt him. And his mother. Was that why he didn't do commitment? Why he didn't do love? Their relationship had been one-sided at best... humiliation warmed her cheeks. Well, if she could think herself into this pain, she could think herself out of it.

"Mr. D'Antoni, we'd almost given up on you."

The sound of the stewardess's voice broke through the tempest of her thoughts. Nico? He lowered himself into the seat beside her, his body all power and strength, his smile taking her blood pressure and raising it a thousand-fold. Their eyes caught and snagged, and his blue gaze drilled into her.

"Are you okay?"

"I am, now." Her voice broke and the tears spilled over. She cried for him. She cried for herself.

"It's over, Abby. It's done."

"I know." She'd stayed strong, but now that he was here... He took her into his arms, and she drank shamelessly of his strength and his scent. He was heaven to her. A heaven she had to steel herself against. It wasn't part of the deal—what happened on the mountain, stayed on the mountain. She could do this. She had to do this. He'd done so much for her and she'd promised him the freedom to walk away, no strings.

It was a freedom she couldn't grant herself. She'd never be free of wanting him—of loving him. But for Nico, she'd put her pain aside and reassure him that she was okay. If she loved him—and she did—she would let him go.

"I'm fine." She straightened up and pulled herself together. "And you're right. It's all over and I can put it behind me now." She sniffed a very un-nun-like sniff and scraped the tears from her face with the back of her hand. "I'm fine, really. Sorry, I was just relieved to see you."

"You thought I'd leave without saying good-bye?" His eyebrows lifted as if to underscore the very small chance of that and an intimate part of her body pulled tight and throbbed with a pulse of its own.

"I did."

The simmering blue of his gaze drew hers like a magnetic field. She didn't want him to see the truth. How much harder would it be if he knew how she felt? Better to bluff it, to keep her weakness to herself. He didn't need to know that even the thought of not seeing him again had broken her heart.

"Abby, I plan to deliver you in one piece to your father as promised."

"And then your job will be done." She infused her tone with a light-heartedness she didn't feel. The loudspeakers crackled and a voice prompted them to tighten their seatbelts. Abby reached for hers and pulled the strap snug. The plane jolted into movement and taxied onto the runway.

"Yes." Black shadows stormed in the summer-sky blue of his eyes and turned them violet.

"I can't thank you enough." Abby swallowed against the knotty lump in her throat.

"It was my privilege, and it was nothing compared with what your father has done for me." His jaw tightened and she turned away, unable to stop the pain from showing on her face. It was nothing? To her, it was everything.

"Abby?"

It was too hard. Too much. She stayed silent, her face averted as they built up speed and hurtled down the runway. The momentum distracted her as the plane lifted into the sky, the upward movement belying the weight that pushed her down. What was wrong with her? She needed to toughen up. To take control. "Yes?"

"I'm beyond sorry the bastard got a shot at you."

"I'm fine." Liar. "And you made sure I wore a protective vest. You did everything in your power to protect me."

"You were hurt by the shackles and the cuffs—the nurse reported back to me. I hope you can forgive me."

"It was nothing." She repeated his words. Nothing compared with the pain that awaited her at the end of this trip.

"It kept you safe, but it wasn't pleasant." He raked his hands through his hair, pushing it back from his forehead.

"He died? The man who took a shot at me?" Her ears hadn't adjust to the increased pressure and her voice sounded hollow and echoey.

"Yes." Nico's jaw locked tight and his expression looked bleak. His thighs flexed and his hands fisted together.

"It wasn't your fault." Abby reached out to comfort him but pulled her hand back.

"No." Nico scowled, and his head tipped back against the headrest.

"He failed… and I testified. And I'm safe. And thanks to you, I'm going home."

"Yes." Nico's eyes closed and he let out a sigh. He looked exhausted.

There was so much Abby wanted to say, to ask, to demand, but she couldn't, not if she was to keep her word. Instead, she too closed her eyes and pretended to sleep. In truth, she savoured his closeness and breathed in his scent and held on to her precious memories.

Nico pulled up outside Abby's home and cut the engine. It was dark, but he didn't plan on seeing her to the door. For one, he'd never been invited into her parents' home. Where before he'd believed himself not worthy of such an invitation, he now realised it was due to Abby's mother's anxiety. If she was afraid to leave the house, she might also be afraid to invite someone from the outside world in.

For two, he needed to think and with Abby's scent driving him to distraction, he couldn't put his words together in any kind of intelligent order. She'd been through a terrible ordeal and he had his brother's death to deal with. She needed the love of her family and Nico needed to focus on the awful tasks ahead. Like telling his parents about the circumstances around Raffaele's death. He'd begun the preliminary tasks needed to get Raffaele's body back to Australia. And he would have to confess to the man who'd given him everything that his own brother—the same miserable arsehole who'd hurt his family before—had tried to kill Abby.

And when Abby learned the truth, she would never want to see him again.

As it was, she needed space and time to recover.

Never had his head felt so chaotic. Somewhere between worrying himself sick that she might get killed and his fear that he could lose her, he'd realised that he couldn't bear to live his life without her.

He'd hoped for a short, blessed moment that Abby might feel the same way… but she was traumatised and upset, and she had every right to be. He would be a fool indeed, to mistake gratitude and relief for something more.

They sat motionless and silent in front of her home which was more of a compound than a house. She was blue blood compared to his black. Whatever delusions he'd harboured, he would do well to remember his roots. This was a woman who had no need for his money or the things he could buy. His body might fit hers to perfection, but his need for her was fiery and dangerous and scared him to bits. Dangerously intense and what if it flared into something worse? Even now, he could feel it. That simmering rage. He wanted her. He loved her and she planned to get out of his car and walk back into her privileged life as if he didn't exist. Damn the woman to hell.

He needed her. He loved her.

She looked at him, the green of her eyes like flame. He'd let her down. He didn't deserve her.

"Good-bye, Nico. I'd ask you in, but my mother wouldn't…" her voice trailed off. Wouldn't like it. Wouldn't like him? Temper stirred in the depths of his soul.

"Abby…" What? An internal voice mocked him. What the hell could he offer her? What the hell did he think she'd say when she learned the truth? Raffaele had ruined any hope of a relationship with her. What good would it do to tell her that he loved her?

She waited, her eyes shining with moisture. Damn. He'd

already hurt her one way or another... and the truth? She was better off without him. That much was clear.

"...I hope you feel better soon. I'm sorry you've been through such a terrible ordeal."

"Thank you." She leaned across to rest her lips softly against his... and detonated a reaction he couldn't control. He took without apology. He took what she offered with every tortured fibre of his being, until he remembered in some dim-witted, slow-to-grow recess of his mind that love wasn't for the likes of him. Walk away. Now. The command became more urgent, more difficult to ignore, until he pushed her away, his body wild with wanting her, his head determined to protect her.

"Go, Abby." His tone was rough. Her lips were bruised and swollen, and he couldn't bear to look at the damage he'd done. "Go, please." Before he did more than kiss her. Before he took what he really wanted with no apology and no finesse.

Why didn't she move?

"Now." His voice cracked like a pistol shot.

He wrenched his door open and dragged himself into the crisp night air. He retrieved her suitcase and plonked it on the nature strip. She was slow to step out of the vehicle and slammed the door with such force that he jerked back.

He couldn't bear it. He couldn't watch as she walked away from the car and out of his life with no hint of indecision.

He couldn't blame her. He'd as good as devoured her with anger. Anger! As if any of this was her fault. He was the one who should have known better. She didn't know the truth. And when she did? She wouldn't want him. She'd walk away and stay away.

He settled himself into the driver's seat and pulled the door closed behind him. Silence. Grab-him-by-the-throat, gut-wrenching silence. He couldn't coordinate his body to do what needed to be done. Breathe. Rev the engine. Drive.

Eyes front. Eyes off the only woman he'd ever love.

Chapter Sixteen

Abby watched the car disappear. Her heart pounded from Nico's thorough assault and every part of her was raw and hurt. For the first time in more years than she cared to remember, she needed her parents. She wanted to be taken into their arms and rocked like a child.

She rang the doorbell. It was ten o'clock in the evening, yet the lights were ablaze, and warmth emanated from within. She was oblivious to the chill in the air and the dark shadows that threatened from every angle.

The door opened and her father engulfed her in his embrace. "Princess. You're home. You're safe. Thank God."

"Yes." Her words were lost in the softness of his Alpaca wool top. She breathed him in, his familiar scent easing into the sore corners of her soul, soothing the sobs that caught in her throat.

Her father held her, and she stood there, powerless to do anything more than absorb his strength.

At last, she lifted her head. "How's Mum?" Her gaze met his... green eyes, the same colour as her own.

"She's fine. I didn't tell her about the trial until I knew you were on your way home. Nico called from the airport to let me know you'd boarded safely and would be home tonight.

Where is he?"

"He didn't stay." She swallowed past the mountain-sized lump in her throat. "I told him about Mum. He knew it would be too much for her."

"Very thoughtful of him. I'll visit his office to express my thanks in person. He's done us an enormous kindness." He pulled her close.

"He's very good at his job." Abby felt like a part of her had been ripped away.

"He's the best. A man of integrity. Come in love. You must be exhausted." He drew her into the hallway and closed the door.

There was a roaring fire in the enormous marble hearth in the living room. He settled her into a soft leather armchair and disappeared into the kitchen. He was back with a hot chocolate in minutes and she sipped it carefully, feeling safe in the familiar setting.

"Your mum's in bed already, but I doubt she's asleep. She's been listening out for you to get back."

"I'll go up in a minute. Thanks, Dad. I appreciate the drink. And thank you for caring."

"I'm very proud of you, princess. I respected your reluctance to go into the witness protection program, but Nico was the best compromise I could come up with. Your life was in danger and I couldn't take the risk."

"Nico was a gentleman in every way."

"He grew up tough on the wrong side of the tracks, but he's a good man."

"What do you mean he's from the wrong side of the tracks?" Her father knew of Nico's past? She crushed her desperate hunger for any crumb of information. She had to put Nico out of her mind. She had to stop wanting what she couldn't have and accept what he'd offered without demanding more. But she wanted more. She wanted it so much it twisted inside her. "You know about his childhood?"

"I'm surprised you didn't ask him." Her father gave her a shrewd look. "I thought he might have shared something of his past with you."

"No." The word battled through the constriction in her throat. "Not much."

"He was brought up in the western suburbs of Sydney, out Blacktown way. He was a smart kid with loads of potential, but his father was a brute and Nico wasn't safe in that environment. But given half a chance, he worked his way clear of the riff raff. He's tough, but honest and hardworking. I couldn't have entrusted your life to anyone else."

Her father was an excellent judge of character. The fact that he'd entrusted her life to Nico spoke volumes about Nico's integrity. Just one of the many things she admired and respected about the man she'd grown to love.

"Thank you, Dad. You were right. My life was in danger. I'm sorry I worried you. You did the right thing and I appreciate it." She had a new appreciation for everything he'd done. His love humbled her. Where before, she'd thought him over-reactive and over-protective, she now recognised the love behind his actions. Perhaps it was less because he believed her to be weak and more because he couldn't bear to lose her. She now had a far better understanding of what it felt like to lose someone she loved.

"You're welcome, princess. Are you ready for bed? Your room's ready." Her father looked older than she remembered, and his shoulders curved like the years weighed on him. His hair had turned silver, and he wore dark-rimmed glasses. Her heart lurched when she realised that he'd aged and that sometime in the future, she would lose him.

She wrapped her arms around him and held him close. "I could sleep for a year."

"Then let's go up, hey? Your mum will be looking forward to seeing you." He patted her back.

"Sure."

Theirs was a comfortable camaraderie. Gone was the anger that so often clouded her judgement around him. Her father loved her. Why he pandered to her mother's fears she'd never know, but maybe love really could transcend all obstacles. Could it? If she loved Nico, was there a chance it could all work out? She hoped with all her heart that was so, but there was a wall between them—more impenetrable and difficult to scale than any physical barrier.

"Abby." Her mother rested against a mountain of pillows. She looked fragile and hauntingly beautiful. Abby had always loved her mother's smell and the softness of her skin. She was like a delicate glasshouse flower, a rare orchid.

"Mum." Abby allowed herself to sink into her mother's fine-boned embrace. She felt stiff to cuddle like a porcelain doll.

"Welcome home, darling."

"Thanks, mum." Abby savoured her mother's sweet scent and sniffed against the sudden rush of tears. She was fine. She would be fine.

"I was so worried when I heard about the trial. I'm so glad it's over."

Abby squeezed her eyes shut against the tears. "Me, too. It was tougher than I expected."

Leaving Nico was tougher than the trial and even now, she

wanted to throw herself at his feet and beg him to stay. What little strength she had leached away, and she yearned to be alone. To grieve. To weep. To succumb to the darkness that pulled at her even now in the warm glow of her parents' love.

"I'm sorry, I'm tired." She wiped at the wayward moisture that leaked from her eyes. "I'll say good-night now and catch up in the morning."

"Of course, darling. I love you. I'm so relieved to have you home." Her mother squeezed her hand.

"I love you, too, mum, and you, dad." She smiled at them both, her love for them swamping her.

"Good-night sweetheart."

She fled to the refuge of her childhood bedroom and threw herself onto the coverlet.

Nico punched the punching bag until his muscles screamed, and then he punched it some more until the sweat rolled down his face and physical pain dulled some of his mental anguish. It had been six weeks since Abby's father had come to his office and thanked him for keeping his precious princess safe and returning her home in one piece.

Well, she may be in one piece, but he sure as hell wasn't. Instead of the usual relief at the end of an encounter with the opposite sex—a kind of grounding as if he'd returned to the fold, intact and ready to prowl some more—he was torn ragged from needing her, near-crippled with desire. Far from healing, every memory near drove him to distraction. He craved her... every touch, every sound, every sight, every taste... her scent bombarded his brain. She'd become a torturous longing he couldn't ease. She'd destroyed him for anyone else. He couldn't even answer another woman's call—beyond a polite text-based decline of any form of intimate invitation.

Night was the worst.

In the mornings, he could take it out on his office punching bag. During the day, he could work like a Trojan horse. In the evenings, he ran as if he could out-run the desire that coiled and snarled in his gut, but at night when he lay down his exhausted head, her phantom touch was there, her hungry kisses, the paradise of her body. More terrible was the lure of her love.

He sensed it like an invisible bind.

If she loved him, his goose was cooked. Because he loved her. Right hook. Left cut. What was he thinking? She didn't love him. Punch. She hadn't contacted him. Hook. What craziness made him think it was even possible? Thwack.

She'd given him nothing to suggest she loved him.

Nothing but the sensual promise of her touch, the heady bewitchment of her kiss. He'd been touched by many a woman. He'd kissed his fair share of them, too. But Abby was… punch… the only woman for him. And therein lay the problem. She wouldn't know the difference between love and lust. She wouldn't recognise what they'd shared as love. She hadn't sampled sex with enough men to know that what they'd shared was the real deal. Punch. She needed experience before she could have that kind of revelation. He couldn't take advantage of her naivety to trap her into something she wasn't ready for. Punch. He couldn't stop the damn need to protect her, which left him between a rock and a hard place. Smack. Not that he was the type to back away from awkward truths. He was the type to face them head on. Punch. Thwack. Smack.

He was an aggressor like his father.

The violence in him subsided and he collapsed against the

bag, holding it close. If he loved her, if he cared at all, he should stay away. But staying away from her was a living hell.

He wanted her love. He wanted her love more than he wanted the zeros after the numbers in his bank account. He'd thought money was the answer, but it turned out it wasn't. Money was a means to an end. A necessary part of life, but far from the icing on the cake.

And Abby wasn't just the icing… she was the icing, the cherry, and the whole damn cake. She was his reason for wanting it. His reason for living.

He reached for his towel and wiped the sweat from his brow. He needed a shower. A long, cold shower; a burning hot shower. He needed to erase the memories that drove him to madness. She'd become an unhealthy obsession.

Where was she? It was a thought that he had a billion times a day. What was she doing? What was going on in her head? Was she okay?

Stop. It had to stop.

Ten hours later, and Nico was on his way to have dinner with his mother. The disappointment in her eyes would be preferable to the emptiness that waited for him at home. His mother had always been his haven. Bullying and bruises had been a constant part of his life, but no pain he'd endured as a child compared with the pain of losing Abby.

He banged on his mother's door and waited a couple of minutes before sliding his key into the lock.

"Hi, Ma," he called. His nostrils filled with the wonderful aroma of spices and baking and he savoured it as he walked the length of the well-lit passage into the open-plan living area at the back. The classic period home in Mosman along the north shore, had been fully renovated before his mum moved in. He'd been careful to retain the character of the place, whilst infusing it with light and space.

"Nico." His mother wiped her floury hands on a towel before she moved to greet him. She took him in her arms. "I'm so happy to see you."

"I'm sorry, mamma. I should have come earlier, but..." Raffaele's funeral had been a small affair. Just the three of them and his parents' grief had been hard to witness. His father's anger had frozen him out, and his mother's tears had fallen like acid-rain against him. He'd needed some space.

"I know. You needed time. We all did." She shooshed him as she would a small boy, her eyes pooling as she leaned back to observe his face before drawing him back into the warmth of her arms. "This wasn't your fault."

"No." His brother had tried to kill him. If not for the bulletproof vest under his clothing, he'd be dead. At his brother's hand. His brother had hated him enough to kill him. It was a truth he couldn't stomach himself let alone share with his mother. She had enough to bear already.

"Something else troubles you."

She was observant as always. He'd never been able to hide anything from her. It was like she could read whatever ailed him in invisible ink on his forehead.

She took his face in her hands and kissed both of his cheeks. "Never mind. I've cooked your favourites. All of them."

There wasn't a drama that food couldn't solve. Good, hearty, home-cooked food was his mother's solution to any ill and he had to hand it to her, the smell of her cooking was the closest thing to heaven since Abby had left him in the cold emptiness of his life without her.

"You're a wonderful woman."

"I am." She pushed him back. Smiled. "You've been working too hard."

"Yes." He settled himself on a stool in front of the vast island bench and his mother pushed two glasses and a bottle of wine towards him.

"Open that, Nico."

"Sure." He took to the task with a heavy heart. He rarely stayed away for long, and he realised with regret that he'd neglected her. It wasn't a comfortable truth. He'd been so absorbed in his own pain that he hadn't considered hers. He poured a small portion.

"Have you seen your father?"

"No." He took a deep gulp of the wine.

"He is angry and grieving, but he loves you."

"I can live without his kind of love."

His mother stopped bustling and turned to him. "When will you forgive him?"

"How could *you* forgive him? He treated you like no man should treat a woman." The angst of the past few weeks roared into his head and he growled with the weight of it. "You should have sent him packing years before you did."

"I loved him, Nico. Nothing will ever change that. He wasn't himself back then with the drinking and the drugs. Poverty takes its toll on a man."

"He used his wife and sons as punching bags. He forced Raffaele into a life of drugs and crime. Raffaele would never have gotten mixed up in the Kercher kidnapping if he'd been raised by a decent man."

"Raffaele made his own choices, the same way you've made yours. He was born and raised in the same house. What's really troubling you?"

"Besides the pall of my brother's death? And my father's blame?"

"Your father has never defined you. You are many times the man your father is, and he's learned from you. You've opened his eyes to a way of life that he thought was beyond his reach. Yes, he resented your interference. Yes, he refused to move from the old house, but you've given us so much. You're a fine man and don't let anyone tell you any differently."

Nico stewed over her words and sipped his wine while his mother spooned hot food into serving dishes. He had nothing to offer Abby. The knowledge cut him deeper than the agony of his brother's betrayal.

"You don't want to talk about it?"

"It's something I need to work out on my own."

"Well, you know where I am. Come. Let's eat."

She gestured towards the table and they sat down together. He felt indulged and loved and it was just what he needed.

"Thank you, mamma. You've outdone yourself here. Your cooking makes a man feel strong."

"You are strong. Your will is strong. You're the man you've chosen to become. You'll be the husband you choose to become and the father you choose to become. I can't see you making the same choices as your papa."

He hoped she was right. Black emotions simmered beneath his carefully contained surface. They scared him, and they'd sure as hell scare Abby.

Or would they? Abby wasn't the type to run from scary. The thought made him chortle. The woman was fearless in the face of bad men and bad situations; yet her body had refused every other man except for him. He felt like Aladdin. Why had he succeeded where others had failed?

She'd been foolhardy to trust someone like him. He was more of a threat to her than the men she'd locked away. But bad men didn't scare her. *Intimacy scared her.*

The thought stopped him in his tracks.

She'd closed her heart to protect herself. He could relate to that. He understood that only too well.

What if she'd walked away because she believed he didn't love her? Not because she didn't want him, but because she feared *he* didn't want *her*? His heart leapt. He looked at the situation—really looked—without the blinding fear. She loved him? She stayed away because she loved him?

His mother's silence was testament to how well she knew him. It was as if she knew the exact moment it was safe to speak.

"Whatever it is, you've worked it out. You're a good man and never forget it."

He loved Abby, and she loved him. The truth was there, as clear as glass and the words in his ears were not as frightful as they'd sounded in his heart.

He was afraid of intimacy and love and commitment. As terrified as any man of taking a woman to be his wife for the rest of his life. Forever was a long time, unless that forever was with Abby, and then it didn't come close to being long enough.

His mother's expression softened, and she smiled, her face lighting from within. "Now, eat my food."

He couldn't stop the warmth. It spread to every frozen corner of his soul. His mother knew him better than any living person. It was a situation he planned to remedy. There was another woman who knew him in a way his mother never could. A woman who'd permeated his mind and body and soul. A woman who'd taken what he'd offered—no promises, no demands—and walked away because she thought that was what he wanted.

It was far from what he wanted.

If she'd gotten what he wanted so wrong, then maybe he'd gotten what she wanted wrong, too. Maybe she hadn't wanted to walk away. There was light on the horizon, and there was only one way to find out.

Chapter Seventeen

Nico had tried to stay away from Abby, but he loved her. Period. He wanted the knots, but Miss Macramé was as good as her word. She'd walked away from him without a backward glance. She was one wise woman as intelligent as she was beautiful.

Nico kept to the shadows at the side of the ballroom, observing Abby as she flitted from table to table in a stunning red sheath dress that clung to her curves and warmed her pale skin. She'd changed since he'd last seen her. She carried herself with a subtle confidence, a maturity she hadn't shown before, a ripening that softened the set of her shoulders and glowed from within. She was beautiful. Hauntingly so. Lusciously so.

His body had been hard at just the thought of seeing her again. The reality of her had his body jammed with tension, a reel of images flickering through his mind like an X-rated movie. He'd been deluded to think he could survive without her.

Abby smiled at a good-looking fellow in evening attire—too suave for Nico's liking—who took her hand and held it for too long. Never had he felt more capable of violence. She was his and the sooner the rest of the world knew it the better. He wanted his ring back on her finger, and his touch—his very possessive and protective touch—back on her body. He waited, his chest heaving.

His father's voice flashed into his head, demanding that he walk away. He didn't deserve this woman. She deserved better than him. He could do harm. Grave harm. Bodily harm. Violence ran in his veins, in his genes.

Worse. His brother had tried to do her harm.

Nico could never hurt her. His urge to protect her was too strong. His love for her was too stark, too desperate. His passion for her, too fiery.

What twisted in his gut was furious indeed. But it was a fury as different from his father's violence as black was to white. It was a longing, a yearning to love her, to lose himself in the heated welcome of her body. Theirs was more than a joining of flesh. It was a meeting of mind and heart and soul. A recognition as ancient as time.

Abby was the only woman for him.

She moved on to another table, and his relief was like a wave of sweet caramel. Another man's touch on her body was like acid on his.

A middle-aged woman stepped up to greet her and gave her a hug. Abby's gaze shifted to the corner where he prowled in the shadows and he felt it like an electric current on his skin.

She took an eternity to excuse herself and cross the room towards him. Her course was punctuated by smiles here and there, and a hug and an air kiss. But there was no smile for him.

Coffee had been served and the night was overdue to finish. He wanted it over. He wanted her to himself.

"Nico?" His name was sharp on her tongue.

"How close are you to being done here?" He couldn't hide

his impatience. The sea-green of her eyes washed over him and perhaps she took pity on him because the rigidity in her spine softened.

"Close enough. I'll get my bag." The short distance to her seat and back was a minefield of social obligations. He felt like a Neanderthal, incapable of verbalising beyond a roar. He wanted to sling her over his shoulder and steal her away. Some primitive part of him thundered and stormed, and his social niceties were in danger of slipping away entirely.

What he'd taken for violence was there in spades.

Desperately contained.

He wanted Abby with every breath, and it took every skerrick of his well-honed discipline to wait. Fear was there, but certainty was stronger. Certainty of purpose. The knowledge that he wanted her in his life. Somehow, he had to convince her that he was worth the risk. Somehow, he had to share his feelings.

Anger had flared in her eyes. Compassion, too. Desire? Yes. But love? He couldn't be sure. After the weeks of wanting and denying himself, these minutes were torture. He'd booked the penthouse suite upstairs, as soon as he'd learned she'd be here, at a fund raiser. The woman was tireless when it came to her cause. The Grand Hyatt in Melbourne was a beautiful, luxury hotel, but he was oblivious to the splendour. His attention was fixed on the vivacious woman he adored. She played hostess like an orchestra played a symphony, with deceptive ease and faultless flow.

Impatience made him pace. He wanted her to himself. Now.

But now turned out to be fifteen minutes later when she finally navigated her way free of the throng.

"Sorry. Tonight, has been brilliant. We've had thousands of

dollars pledged. Just think what we can do with that funding." She couldn't keep the passion from her voice or the excitement from her face. Nico couldn't keep his lips from hers. He drew her into a shadowy recess and dragged her body against his, lowering his mouth to within a breath of hers.

"Abby, I need to kiss you."

"Nico, I thought…"

Whatever she thought was completely lost on him because even as she said the words, she leaned in and closed the gap. Their lips fused and he was lost… her kiss drawing him in with every intimate stroke and slide of her tongue. If kisses could speak, this one roared with desperate words and a raging appetite.

Abby's body moulded against his and time stalled. The closer she pressed, the deeper he sank into the allure of her kiss. His hands tangled in her hair and he drew her body ever tighter against the contour of his. She plundered and took, and with every gasp, every whimper, every insatiable groan, her arms tangled tighter around his neck and drew him deeper into the magic she spun.

Demanding. Taking. Giving. Sharing.

Nico was lost. Lost to time and place. Lost to everything except the siren-like call of her body against his. To the pain-gilded pleasure of Abby finally in his arms. He was hard. Harder than he'd ever been and if they didn't stop…

The thought brought him back from the brink, but his call for order took time to reach his stampeding senses. Abby whimpered her displeasure, her reluctance to follow his lead.

"We need to talk." His words were whisper soft, weakened like the rest of him. He wanted to do this right. Not molest her. Not take what he wanted like a common thug never mind how willing she was.

The flames eased but the passion she ignited was not of the extinguishable kind. It was a lesson he'd been slow to appreciate. He didn't think he'd ever get enough of her. The more he tasted, the more he wanted, the more he needed.

His breath was short, and he battled the boorish demands of his body.

Abby nodded, her gaze colliding with his. There was desire and the shadow of something more. He wanted to know what it was. What did she hide? Not in a cowardly way, more like a warrior woman wielding a shield.

She nestled against him and he breathed her in with unashamed delight, his eyes closing to better savour the heaven of her there, in his arms.

With his pulse banging in his ears, Nico drew Abby towards the bank of lifts. The ballroom was near empty, and the wait staff had finalised the pack up.

"I organised the penthouse so we could have some privacy to talk."

Her raised eyebrow questioned his motives, but she would just have to trust him on that. If their talk led to other things, well and good, but first he needed to get his thoughts in order.

A whole new battalion of feelings had him under siege, and he wasn't sure where to begin.

The feel of Abby's hand safely in his was a paradise beyond pleasure. How could something so simple conjure such joy? It spoke of trust and faith, two emotions he treasured above all else. Two emotions that didn't come easily to him.

Except with Abby.

He slid the key card into the lock... there was the sweetness of her scent and the feel of her hand in his. He wanted to remember this moment forever. He wanted and feared what would come next. A life together or a life apart? The truth lay between them. And once he'd told her—everything—the choice would be hers.

The suite was cool and contemporary in design, with a wall of windows that displayed an exposé of lights like a magic carpet below. Abby settled her bag on the plush leather couch, her hands trembling slightly as they twisted together. There was a posy of pink roses on the table and dancing flames in the fireplace. The room had a sense of warmth and elegance.

A bottle of champagne rested in a bucket of ice and when he reached for it and eased the cork out of the top. He poured a small amount into a glass and passed it across to her. She eyed the bowl of chocolate dipped strawberries and the green of her eyes turned to frost. He'd wanted everything to be perfect but now that he saw the room through her eyes, he realised he'd gone too far. The room looked set for seduction. Hell. He'd wanted to do this right. He'd wanted to make her feel special, not cheap.

"Nico, why are you here?" Abby's face was now a carefully arranged mask and he had no idea what thoughts churned behind it.

"Has this got something to do with my father?" She lowered the glass to the coffee table with a disappointed look on her face.

"Abby, I'm not here because of your father."

Her brow creased with questions. "Then, why?" Her gaze shifted to the lavish suite and a new layer of ice formed.

Six weeks of agonising silence. Did Nico think she was just going to slide back into his arms? Did he think he could just drop into her life for a quick rendezvous whenever the urge took him? Her eyes dropped to the champagne and strawberries. Woo her back into his bed for some fiery sex only to be gone the next moment? That was probably how his liaisons typically went.

And she'd melted into his arms. If tonight's reaction was anything to go by, his thinking was right. The thought brought an erotic jolt to the already simmering sensation between her thighs. His kiss had told her loud and clear that he still desired her, but she'd heard nothing from him since he'd left her. She'd tried to put their relationship into perspective, but she'd failed dismally. If she gave in to this yearned-for moment, she'd reopen a festering wound. She rallied her defences. A crumb from a towering cake of temptation bestowed upon her at his beck and call?

He was here. Wasn't that what she'd longed for? But maybe he just wanted her back in his bed. She knew better than to think he could love her. She knew his mode of operandi. Love them and leave them. She wasn't any different from the other woman he'd bedded. She got that. She understood it now, better than she had before.

He'd driven away and stayed away. He'd washed his hands of her.

Women who shared his bed didn't share it for long.

No way would she be a convenient fling for him when he was in town. She'd rather not have him at all. Not when she loved him. The thought cut like a blade.

She wanted his love. She wanted forever. And this? This was not nearly enough. But to be this close and to look into the stormy depths of his eyes? She was pathetic. Weak. And she wouldn't stand for it.

She loved, where he desired. She wanted forever, where he wanted a night together. She wanted… her eyes dropped from the violet blue of his eyes, to the treacherous line of his jaw and the firm edge of his mouth. Memories of his kiss rioted inside her and drew him closer as if the earth had shifted on its axis. She steeled her spine and readied herself to decline whatever tawdry proposition he planned to offer.

Better to live without him than to lose him over and over again. It didn't fit with who she was, who she'd become, who she wanted to be. She was worth more than what Nico had to offer.

"I'm sorry. I was wrong to walk away. Crazy to stay away." Nico reached out and took Abby's hand. Her skin was soft and cool. He needed to connect, to touch. "I owe you an apology."

"*I* owe you my life." Tears welled in her eyes and clung to her lashes.

"No, Abby. I owe you more than you could ever owe me."

"How can you say that?"

"I'm torn between wanting to protect you and wanting to take everything I need and more. I'm not proud of where I come from and I've spent most of my adult life trying to forget my childhood and put it behind me."

He couldn't mess this up. It was too important. She was too important.

"Back then, all those years ago, when you thought I rejected you… I wanted you so much… so much more than I should have."

"You hated me." The old hurt was etched on her face.

"No, I hated *me*. I was hell bent on being something more than what I was, and I resented the privilege in your life. I resented how your father loved you and treated you like the most precious thing in the world, while mine knocked me around and used me as a punching bag."

Maybe the seed of his love for her had taken root all those years ago. He brought her hands to his lips.

"That wasn't your fault."

He wondered what he could ever have done to deserve the love of such a beautiful woman. She was good to his bad. Pure to his sin. White to his black.

"We don't get a choice about who our parents are." She held his gaze and her green eyes shone like polished turquoise. "The only choice we have is what we make of ourselves and our life. Look at what you've achieved. Look at the incredible man you've become."

He felt it. That aura of warmth, that magical mantel that settled around him when he was close to her. He liked who he was in her eyes. He liked the man she saw. The man he became in her arms.

And he couldn't accept what he hoped was her love until she knew the truth and she chose to love him anyway.

He'd walked away from her. Hell, he'd raced away from her like she'd grown horns and a barbed tail. No wonder she was wary. Wary. He didn't blame her. But this time, he wasn't leaving until he told her everything. All of it, right down to his unworthy declaration of love. Hell, she'd be forgiven for thinking she'd been wooed by the devil.

It was a compulsion he couldn't stop. He wanted her to know him. Really know him. If she knew the worst and loved him anyway, then maybe he could believe they had a future. And he wanted her to know that he loved her.

He settled her beside him on the couch, his grip tight on her hands.

"When I was a kid, I learned to look out for myself, to think fast. My mother and I took the brunt of my father's violence, which was worse when he was stoned." Abby's eyes welled with tears and he yearned to take her in his arms, but he was determined to say what he needed to say.

"My older brother, Raffaele, went to prison for twenty years because of me—when I was twelve years old, I overheard him talking with his mates about something they'd done, and I went to the police." Nico took a deep breath and steadied himself. She needed to know it all including the danger he'd put her in. "Raffaele was released from prison earlier than I expected and shortly before we headed to New Zealand. It was Raffaele who planted the bug in our room, and he planned to kill us. We would have died in our sleep if we'd stayed there the night we left." Abby's eyes widened but she didn't interrupt. "When I spoke with the staff at the Chateau, they said they'd received a tip off about damage to the flue and they found a serious carbon monoxide leak. I remember now how yellow the flame looked after the fire evacuation." He lifted her hands to his mouth and ran his lips over her soft skin. "I've since discovered that Raffaele's motorcycle club buddies had connections with the paedophile group you exposed."

Abby reached out and squeezed his hand. The compassion in her eyes was more than he deserved.

"There's more." Nico took a deep breath. "Raffaele was the man who took a shot at us when we were in Bangkok. The job wasn't done, and he couldn't allow you to testify."

"But what did he have to do with Project Karma?" He saw the moment she made the connection and her hands lifted to her mouth. Her eyes were wide with shock. His brother was dead.

"I'm so sorry, Nico."

"He chose to kill himself."

"He was still your brother. And I'm sorry for your loss."

Raffaele didn't deserve Abby's sympathy and neither did he. The negative words bellowed in his head, but he refused to listen. This was Abby and if anyone could forgive him, she could. Whether she did or not was up to her. But there was more to tell.

He reached for his champagne and took a deep gulp. Setting the glass back down on the table, he steeled his spine.

"Twenty years ago, when I was twelve and you were only five, I overheard Raffaele and his bikie mates talking about a woman and a child that they'd kidnapped and locked away in our garage. They were boasting about the size of the ransom and how it would set them up for life."

Abby showed no sign of recognition about the kidnapping she'd endured. "I went to the police and when they raided our home..." He reached out for her hands and squeezed. "...they saved you and your mother."

She leapt to her feet and shook her head. "No, I'd remember...' He saw the moment she realised the truth. "My father told me it that wasn't real. It was a bad dream. A nightmare..." She sank back down onto the couch and Nico took her hands in his.

"I'm sorry, Abby. Bob thought he was helping you." Her hands shook and Nico sat in silence while she digested the truth of it.

"It's because of my brother that your dad is over-protective. It's because of my brother and his mate that your mother suffers from post-traumatic stress disorder. His mate sexually assaulted your mother—in front of you. He went to prison for his trouble, but recently died from a combination of alcohol and drugs." Nico took a deep breath. This was the part where he deserved her hatred. He'd known what was buried beneath her anxiety around sex and he hadn't told her. "I should have told you, but I have your father to thank for the man I am today. He paid for my schooling and mentored me while I built up my business. Your father made me promise not to tell you the truth about what happened, because he wanted to protect you. I spoke with him before I came down to see you..."

"Because if we're to move forward you don't want this kind of secret between us?"

"I know I don't deserve your forgiveness, but it wasn't my secret to tell. When you told me, you freeze up when you get close to a man... I figured you were probably suffering from some form of post-traumatic stress after what happened to you all those years ago. I should have told you. I could have helped you to make sense of those feelings without needing to..." Hell, he should have told her before he'd taken advantage of her trust in him.

"But you promised my father you wouldn't tell." Abby nodded. "And when I was a teenager and I tried to kiss you, you thought you weren't good enough for me because of what your brother did."

"Yes. I grew up in a steaming crap-pile and you deserved, you deserve..." He squeezed her hands and forced himself to look into the luminous depths of her eyes. "A far better man than me."

When Abby cradled his jaw with her palm and drew him towards her mouth, he fought the compulsion to take what she offered. "I want to be the man I am in your eyes. Not like my father or my brother."

How could she bear to love him now? What if she couldn't? He shouldn't have come. He should have stayed the hell away from her.

"Nico, I can see what you're doing to yourself. This wasn't your fault. Your brother made his choices. He did his time, but he didn't learn from his mistakes. Even at twelve years of age, you chose to do the right thing. Your brother was a grown man, and he chose to do the wrong thing. You're not like him. You're not like your father."

"What if I am?"

"I don't believe it. I can't believe it. You protect people. That's what you do. You've been protecting others since you were a child. No child should be mistreated by those who are supposed to care for them. You deserve to be loved. All of us do. You're not your brother. Or your father."

"I hurt you. Five years ago."

There. He'd put it on the table. Their past. How could she forgive him for how he'd treated her? He'd handled her proposition badly. He accepted that now.

"As awful as it was back then, you helped me to see the truth. I was a pampered princess... I was indulged and there was a good chance I would have turned into one of the spoilt girls I hung out with. I was trying so hard to fit in and I couldn't see what was important. You opened my eyes to that. It is because of you that I sought a job that matters." Her words were a whisper, but her eyes burned like molten jade.

"You were young." The memory of her disappointment and her shame lanced his heart. At the time, her pain had been the only thing that had endeared her to him... she'd been criminally attractive. Beauty to his beast.

"In hindsight, it was a blessing in disguise."

So that was how she viewed it. Relief infused his veins, and he sank back onto the couch.

"It changed my life in a good way. If I hadn't travelled to Thailand, I wouldn't have met Gary and his group or discovered how entrenched the problem of child exploitation was. I couldn't believe that innocent children were being pawned for money. I ended up helping them and got involved with the Project Karma group. By saving others, I saved myself and that was thanks to you."

Courageous green eyes held his. Still, he couldn't quite hope that she could love him after all he'd shared. His emotions rose in his throat until he thought he'd choke on them. He made no effort to hide his desperate need for her, but it was her love he craved. The most important moment in his life and all he could do was grapple for breath.

Abby's face was etched with emotions as raw as his. Shadows. He wanted those shadows gone. He wanted her. All of her. Every dark, shadowy corner of her lit with love.

The air between them swirled with an audible pulse. Nico growled and scooped her into his arms, drawing her into a worshipping kiss.

Abby felt like a goddess. His tasting was desperate and demanding, and his touch was fretful like he wanted to savour every living piece of her all at once.

"Abby…"

His voice resonated against her lips. His groan was guttural and protracted as he eased away, but his mouth returned to hers like he couldn't bear the distance.

"Kiss me." She spoke against his upper lip where the smooth

velvet of his lips bordered with the more rugged terrain of his face. She sank into the promise of a kiss that was both carnal and sensual.

It was a kiss that stole the truth from her... she loved him, and it was a truth that left her exposed and vulnerable. Weak.

She was weak with wanting him. Weak with her need for him. She had to toughen up. This was a man who endowed women with one hundred and ten percent of his attention when they were in his arms and then walked away. Without communication for long, torturous weeks. She forced herself to rein in the flat out, thundering, dust-billowing gallop, that headlong bolt of her senses towards a cliff edge of regret. What she wanted and what he wanted were polar opposites. She'd do well to remember it.

"Abby. I'm not done."

A moment ago, she hadn't cared. She'd wanted him, dangers and all. Dangers she'd sensed in him, leashed and shackled. She didn't want his control, his protection, his safe keeping.

She wanted his love.

Hell, this was the hardest thing she'd ever done.

"I need to go." The words were there, between them, before she'd censored or considered them in any way. It was a truth she recognised at once. She should go. To stay was insanity. Not now. Not now, when she knew she wanted it all.

All or nothing.

"Damn it, Abby. There's no way in Hades I'm going to let you go before I've said what I need to say."

Blue flame stayed her movement and temper flashed in his eyes. She sank back into her seat, the momentary rush of strength gone. And she saw it. The violence he was capable of. It slowed the thump of her heart in her chest and she gathered her defences, her senses ragged.

He raked his hands through his already dishevelled hair and her heart lurched. She loved the way he did that. The way he looked at her as if she were the most beautiful woman in the world, as if he had to fight his desire for her, as if just looking at her was enough to physically pain him.

Well good, she hoped he suffered. She waited while he organised his thoughts.

His gaze burned into hers. "Abby, I've never wanted a woman as much as I want you."

She'd heard enough. She didn't need to hear anymore. She saw it on his face. Desire. Lust. It wasn't enough. It didn't come close to being enough.

"Nico, don't. I can't be with you and then watch you walk away—speed away—like you can't leave fast enough. I know you can't love me, and I understand that, but I can't do this over and over. It hurts too much."

She struggled to her feet and twisted away from him. She had to go, while she still could. She'd known his terms going in. They were terms she couldn't accept. Not now. Not when she knew she wanted his love. She just had to toughen up. Get strong. Deny herself.

"Abby, please let me finish."

Abby stilled. She didn't want to hear what he had to say. Self-preservation demanded that she leave before he shattered her completely.

If she didn't get out of here now, her emotions would overflow and with them would come a *declaration of love*. A declaration he didn't want to hear. A declaration he'd rejected before.

She struggled to draw breath, a band tightening around her

chest. She didn't think she could face the shame of his rejection again. Once in a lifetime was more than any woman should have to endure.

"I need to go." She blindly groped for her bag, tears welling and distorting her vision.

Chapter Eighteen

"Abby, please hear me out. I'm begging you." Nico's heart banged in his chest and anger snarled, savage, but shackled.

Fear flashed across Abby's face and Nico felt it within him. Violence… black and dangerous. But far from wanting to hurt her, he wanted to love her. The sight of her pain was intolerable

"Five years ago, when I told you I didn't believe in love, I was angry, and I said things I shouldn't have."

"I know you can't love me, but I won't accept anything less." Her voice snagged. "I can't be your casual plaything."

"Abby, without you, I'm useless. I can't function. I can't sleep. I can't bear the emptiness of every day, but loving you scares me senseless." What the hell had she said? "Damn it, Abby. What we shared was far from a casual fling."

"Loving me scares you?" She'd stopped rushing away and the relief left him weak.

"Yes." Fear raced through his veins. Had he just told her he loved her? Kind of.

"You told me that love was the stuff of fairy tales. That you didn't expect a princess like me to understand the first thing about the real world."

"I said a lot of things I wish I hadn't, but you've proved me wrong. Very wrong."

"What are you saying?" Her eyes overflowed with tears, so many tears, so much pain. His heart lurched and he leapt to his feet and pulled her into his arms.

"I'm sorry, Abby. I'm not even close to being worthy of you. You deserve someone so much better than me, but I can't stand the thought of another man being anywhere near you. I love you so much and I can't tell you how much I need to know whether you love me, too."

Nico shook like a leaf and Abby held on tight as her heart roller-coasted and soared with hope.

"Why do you think I deserve better?" She held her breath.

"I'm not worthy of you, but I love you more than any other man could." Raw emotion drowned the light in his eyes, leaving them midnight black.

She ached for the small boy inside him, and her compassion brought fresh tears to her eyes. No child should have to grow up with abuse and neglect. No man should have to take the weight of his brother's bad deeds. Nico was not like his family and the fact that he wasn't spoke volumes about the man that he was.

His muscles bunched across his shoulders and his back bowed towards her, his arms wrapping tightly around her. What did he think? That she couldn't love a man whose father had beat him? Who'd grown up with disadvantage and poverty?

Anger sparked as she registered the insult. Did he think she'd turn up her privileged nose and walk away because he hadn't grown up in Mosman? Or Double Bay? Or some other wealthy suburb? He didn't think much of her if he believed that could make a difference.

He pulled away and forehead creased. "If you marry me, you marry my family. My gene pool will mix with yours in our children." His warning was razor sharp. A muscle ticked in his jaw and his eyes bored into hers, exposing a myriad of worries.

Marry? Their children? A child. An image flashed into her mind of a small boy with an olive complexion, dark hair, and a smile to die for… and her anger lost some of its sting.

"Shame on you for thinking that would make a difference to how I feel." She glared at him, but he glared straight back. He wasn't afraid to challenge her. He was honest to the core. A man she respected and loved more than words could say. "I appreciate the warning, but I don't remember you asking me to marry you." Her words were whisper soft, but steely. His love was there on his face and in that moment, she saw it. She knew it. She believed it.

"I love you, Abby. I love you with beat of my heart. I want to be with you until the very last one, and then I want to share our eternity. Marry me, please. I'm begging you. I can't live without you." He fumbled in his pocket for her diamond engagement ring. "I believe this belongs to you."

Abby couldn't breathe. She couldn't speak for a long moment. Her heart sang and cried and danced, but her emotions strangled the words she needed to say.

But it must have been there in her eyes because his tension ebbed away. His hard expression softened and the tempest that stormed in the blue of his eyes cleared.

Finally, she wrestled her words into order. "I love you, too, with all of my heart and more." Tears fought with her smile and she settled into the heaven of his gaze, and a kiss that spoke of promises and always and forever and yours.

And it didn't stop there, or at least only for a moment when Nico eased back from their passionate tasting to gasp. "Is that a yes?"

"Yes, that's a yes. Yes, yes and YES."

"Even though our children will carry the risk of my family's genes?" He lifted her hand and slipped the ring into place.

"They'll carry your genes and mine." Abby lifted her ring to the light with a smile. She loved this ring, almost as much as she loved Nico and the familiar weight of it on her hand was like coming home. Mr. and Mrs. Bortoli... D'Antoni.

Nico grinned and Abby felt the zipper of her dress being slowly released along the length of her spine—the fabric falling loose—his hands impatient as he pushed the garment over her shoulders and away from her breasts.

His hands were greedy, and she welcomed them.

Never would she be able to get enough of his touch. His eyes held hers with the promise of paradise. The promise of forever. The promise of love. And his hands were reverent. Nico was the only man she'd ever loved. Strong and gorgeous and intelligent and honed from rock as primeval as the mountain that had brought them together.

"So, my beautiful, soon-to-be wife... if you're willing to accept the dangers of loving me, can we take this to the bedroom?"

She couldn't stop the smile of consent.

"I'm yours, anywhere, anytime." She kicked off her shiny red stiletto heels and Nico ran his magical touch down the length of her leg. Far from wanting to leave, she wanted to get naked. As soon as physically possible.

"I like the sound of that."

"I like the feel of that." She loved how wicked she felt in his arms. How irresistibly sexy.

Nico picked her up with a growl and strode to the bedroom where he threw her mercilessly onto the massive bed. She fought with his clothing and sought to remove it with distracted speed. A feminine purr of satisfaction rose in her throat as she revealed his chest, honed and perfect, and lower, lower to that part of him she desired most. He finished the strip in record time, and she pulled him close, her hands reaching for his tight rounded buttocks, his skin olive brown to her pristine white.

As far as foreplay went, she was done. Fully ready. Fully wet and swollen with need.

Their coupling was far from gentle.

At last, he unleashed the beast that she'd always sensed he held in check. That last vestige of forbidden territory. He took her with rapacious greed; with a love that was both dangerous and safe. He took her to mountainous heights... to rugged, treacherous, ancient ground where primal needs raged, and civility was nothing but a veil to be torn down and trampled. Flames burned and devoured everything in their path. Never had Abby felt so harried, so frenzied in her rush to the heavens. Their joining was complete, soul-deep, and earth-defying.

Here was love. Naked and true and whittled down to its most elemental form.

Abby's body gripped Nico's like a velvet fist. She matched him thrust for thrust and took him to the verge of madness.

Never had he imagined it could be like this.

Never had he allowed himself to let go, to lose himself in a woman so completely.

He soared with the blissful wonder of it. There was nothing between them but love and desire and all things good. No secrets. No doubts. And it was a moment he would cherish forever. A paradise beyond anything he deserved, but Abby had given him the gift of her love.

Nothing transcended the sound of her rapture and the erotic clutch of her body as it crested wave upon wave—it tore his control to shreds and he plunged after her into that place that was theirs alone.

Never had he flown so high.

Never had he shattered so completely. Never again would he be the man he'd been. Abby loved him and her light outshone any darkness that might linger inside him.

His mouth preyed on hers and she hungered right back. Never would he stop wanting her. Theirs was a passion as endurable as time. Her love was a gift, both healing and liberating. Elation drove their kiss—a glorious plundering that had him hard and throbbing and wanting her all over again. She took him deeper, her mouth on his, her body coaxing him to move. This time their pace was slower and more sensual, a quiet simmer rather than a furious boil. He rolled her over and she lay astride, her pace leading his. She took what he offered and gave in return, and their pleasure increased a thousand-fold with the raw emotions that shared.

When their pace began to grow and to flower, Nico gloried in the magic she spun with the sensual glide of her body over his. And he knew without a doubt, their love would endure.

And when the storm abated and they lay sated and at peace in each other's arms, they found heaven indeed. He would protect her with his life. He was the CEO of the largest security company in Australia. He was the best man for the job. And

Abby was the only woman for him.

Epilogue

Abby observed herself in the full-length mirror. Her dress was understated, but elegant, the fabric a precious ivory silk that whispered over her body as she stepped into it.

She looked beautiful, and radiant with love and happiness. She couldn't wait for the ceremony to begin, to make the vows that would bind her and Nico for the rest of their lives.

Their wedding day.

No paparazzi.

No guests beyond their respective parents and their closest friends. She had no desire for a high society circus, and she wanted her mother to feel comfortable. The wedding celebrant would conduct the ceremony on the terrace of her parent's house.

The day was as gloriously perfect as the piercing blue of Nico's gaze, which guarded her safely across the short distance between them. Abby was oblivious to everything but the love that shone in his eyes like a trillion diamonds.

The sun sparkled on the bay behind him, a sparkling expanse that haloed the man whose reverent expression took her heart and her soul. His smile pulled at more intimate places and when his hand reached for hers, the connection was as binding as the vows they planned to make.

Here was the man she loved. The man who loved her.

The ceremony was poignant and perfect, and they made promises that would last a lifetime.

The luncheon that followed was happy and intimate. Abby watched as Nico spoke with his father and savoured the knowledge that they'd made steps towards healing the pain of the past. Her own father was jovial and the three of them were gunning with enthusiasm about the current economic opportunities.

Nico's mother and her own couldn't have been more different but they complemented each other, and Abby felt truly blessed to have them both in her life. She adored Nico's feisty mum and revelled in her strength. This was the kind of mother she wanted to be.

And now that she had a better understanding of the trauma her own mother had suffered they were able to support each other and move forward. The tentacles of the past may never fully leave her, but with Nico's love, she felt strong and shielded and safe.

It was a happy and seamless melding of very different families from very different backgrounds.

"Mrs D'Antoni. Are you ready to go?" Nico gathered her close and she knew she'd willingly follow him to the ends of the earth and beyond, should he dare to take her there.

"Where are we headed?"

"Somewhere safe—as safe as it can be with a seismograph on the counter." His blue gaze held hers and she grinned.

Mr. and Mrs. D'Antoni.

And she couldn't wait for their second honeymoon to begin.

* * *

Thank you so much for reading *Bachelor on Guard!* I hope you enjoyed Abby and Nico's story. Bachelor on Guard is from my 'Beauty and the Bachelor' box set—a collection of standalone stories based on the Beauty and the Beast trope!

Abby and Nico find love and healing together, and their connection for me, was a strong one. The setting is a powerful part of this story and New Zealand has the most unearthly but beautiful scenery. I first visited Mt. Ruapehu in the mid-1990s. After a brief afternoon ski on our first day at Turoa, we saw a massive mushroom cloud and couldn't believe the mountain had erupted. We didn't get to ski Mt. Ruapehu for the rest of the week but we saw Rotorua and got amazing footage of an active volcano. I have a snapshot in my mind of the Chateau Tongariro Hotel which rests at the base of the volcano, lit by the sun with the mountain spewing steam behind it. Years later, in 2012, I booked a couple of nights there with a girlfriend and we tried again to ski Mt. Ruapehu, but it wasn't to be. The mountain was closed due to bad weather, so we played pool and enjoyed the historic Hotel. For me, the mountain remains unconquered, but Abby and Nico struck it lucky. I hope you enjoyed travelling there with them.

If you enjoyed *Bachelor on Guard,* I'd really appreciate an honest review on your Amazon website of choice and/or on Goodreads: https://www.goodreads.com/book/show/4 1014887-desert-prince-scandalous-affair. Authors rely on readers' reviews to stand out (hopefully in a good way)!

And if you'd like to join my newsletter and receive a free welcome gift (Bachelor on Trial), I'd love to see you at: https://dl.bookfunnel.com/lzmhskru7g

I'd love to hear from you!

You can find me at www.lexigreene.com.au.

Or on facebook at www.facebook.com/lexi.greene.75 or www.facebook.com/lovelexigreene.

Warmest regards,

Lexi xx

About the Author

Lexi is an Australian author who loves to write powerful, passionate and provocative stories. She writes romance in the early morning and works as a paediatric neuropsychologist by day. A happily married mum of two teens, a parrot and a puppy, she loves to escape into a good story. She is a firm believer that a bath, a green tea and chocolate take a good book and make it perfect.

Lexi is a member of Romance Writers of Australia and Romance Writers of America; and is a huge fan of Margie Lawson's Writer's Academy.

Lexi loves a good happily ever after...

Also by Lexi Greene

Bachelor on Trial
When Tony Radcliff joins Forbes lawyers, career-driven Scarlet O'Connor finds she has competition for the coveted senior associate position.

And Tony has a couple of aces up his sleeve. Like his surf-sculpted body, which plays havoc with Scarlet's 'all work and no play' plans for partnership. And his brother, who holds the key to a secret from her past.

When Scarlet and Tony start steaming up the office windows, there's no doubt they're playing with fire. But there can only be one winner, so who gets burned?

https://books2read.com/Bachelor-On-Trial

Bachelor on Board

Success is the best revenge.

And Amber Reed is determined to make her new show—Bachelor on Board, Australia—outshine the one her ex stole from her, even if that means facing the worst mistake of her life, Nathan Moretti.

Nathan needs a wife to protect the family fortune from his gold-digger stepmother and his job should be easy with twenty-four beautiful women to choose from. Right?

Not when the only woman he's ever loved is the one behind the camera and her success relies on him finding love with someone else, on screen, on schedule, as promised.

https://books2read.com/Bachelor-On-Board

Shatterproof

Emily Stone, an internationally successful model on the brink of supermodel stardom, appears to have it all. All, except love, because Emily wants the kind of man who isn't fooled by the pretty. She wants the kind of love that's big enough and true enough to include her disabled sister and dysfunctional mother.

Nick was an A-list actor in tinsel town with a super-sized ego until a tragic car accident stole his wife, his unborn child, and his gilded career, leaving him physically and emotionally scarred.

When wintry French Island brings these two wayward souls home, shared childhood memories aren't enough to bridge the deep divide forged by their adult lives and choices.

That is until Carmie, Emily's delightful Down Syndrome sister, weaves her special kind of magic. Can Carmie's boundless love and infectious joy help them to heal their broken hearts or will the glamour of Emily's work-world whisk her away?

https://books2read.com/Heart-of-Glass-Shatterpoof

Once Upon A Christmas Wish

Jenn Adams is determined to tick off her bucket list and face her past nemeses—learning to ski and a man named Brad.

Brad Oregon is the only man she's ever loved. His chocolate eyes. His to-die-for smile. His toned body. His very toned body.

But Brad's reputation with women is almost as renowned as his ski-racing success. Now a ski instructor in beautiful Whistler, he's as difficult to resist as the scenery! What the hell. Life is short. A two week holiday romance should suit them both perfectly. Right?

https://books2read.com/Once-Upon-A-Christmas-Wish

Desert Prince, Scandalous Affair

There is nothing Zahidah's Prince Rashid bin Ra'ed Al Shahid won't do to safeguard his family's honour and his kingdom's future.

And there is nothing Jemma Mason won't do to protect her daughter, Sami, the result of a crazy one-night connection with a dark, handsome cliché in a Sydney bar.

When Sami needs a bone marrow transplant to save her life, Jemma must travel to Zahidah and face the prince who has no idea he's a father. But when Princess Aminah, Rashid's sister, steps in and saves Sami's life (and Jemma's secret), there is nothing Jemma won't do for Aminah including rescuing her from an arranged marriage she dreads.

When Aminah is abducted, Rashid's carefully laid plans for Zahidah's future are put in jeopardy. Prince Rashid wants answers and his questions deliver him to Jemma, the irritatingly familiar woman who befriended his sister.

How long can Jemma keep up her charade and deny an attraction as enduring as the ancient sands? Or will she once again surrender to her handsome desert prince and a scandalous affair?

https://books2read.com/Desert-Prince-Scandalous-Affair